The Seven
Levels of Sin

Book One: Spark

S.L. PEARCE

The Seven Levels of Sin: Spark
First Published August 2023

This is a work of fiction.

Names, characters, business, events, and
incidents are the products of the author's
imagination.

Any resemblance to actual persons, living or
dead, or actual events is purely coincidental.

Whilst the Great Plague did happen, as far as
we know…it was not caused by supernatural
entities, but it did indeed cause devastation
and the loss of lives. You will also find that
famous brands/bands may be mentioned –
these are owned by the respective owners
and as such we do not claim to have
copyright over these.

This is a work of fiction.

DEDICATION

I wish to extend my heartfelt gratitude to my family, who have been my pillars of strength and support. It has been eight years since I started this story, and their unwavering support has played an integral role in bringing this to fruition.

To my parents:
You have been my guiding light, demonstrating the power of hard work and how to have a positive outlook in accomplishing great things.

To my sister:
Who has been a constant source of inspiration, fueling my creative fire and urging me to remain imaginative.

To my husband and daughter:
I am indebted to you for your unwavering belief in me, for anchoring me to my goals and reminding me of my purpose in storytelling.

The Seven Levels of Sin

Book One: Spark

S.L. PEARCE

The Seven Kingdoms

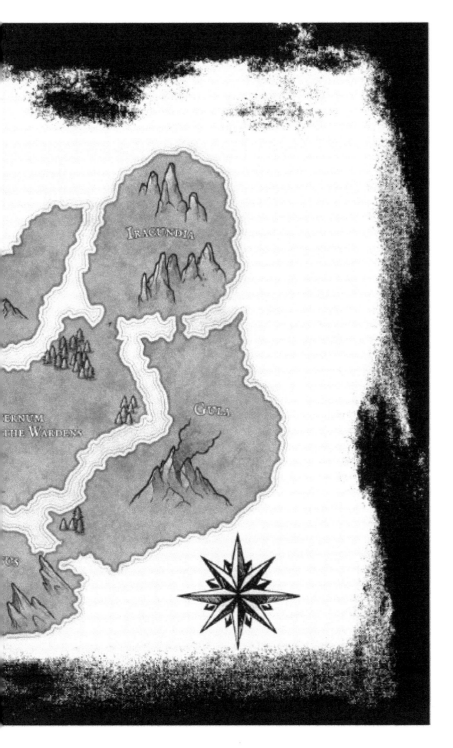

Chapter List

When she rises, Hell fire
will surely follow…
-Book of the Ancient Artefacts-

Prologue

Year 1600

The 1600s were a time of chaos and destruction. Particularly in Europe, as kingdoms waged war against each other in a desperate bid for power. The conflict had already taken a heavy toll on the people, with cities being reduced to rubble and countless lives lost. But the worst was yet to come, as the deadly war began to spread through the population, claiming innocent victims and earning the moniker of the *'Great Plague'*.

As if the loss of life and destruction of property weren't enough, there was also the looming threat of demonic forces at play. Power hungry and determined demons were plotting big moves as they hunted for more souls.

Wardens, individuals tasked with hunting and eliminating demons, had infiltrated the upper echelons of society, gaining positions of power and influence in an effort to purge any trace of evil from history. They had become virtually untouchable, holding exclusive seats on councils, and wielding immense power over the fate of others.

Despite the chaos and disorder, there were still leaders who worked tirelessly to bring peace and stability to the realm. They knew that in order to prevent such a catastrophic event from occurring again, they had to put an end to the never-ending cycle of warfare and strive for cooperation between nations. But there were others who remained intent on taking the throne, believing that their ascension would appease the mythical entity known as the Deus Inferni.

On the 6th of June 1666 the tables turned. The air was filled with jubilation and happiness as the Wardens had successfully negotiated and secured a treaty amongst all of the Kings and Queens of Hell, putting an end to the years of strife and conflict. Despite their previous antagonism towards each other, the seven royal leaders set aside their differences and agreed on a pattern of governance that would alternate every seven years. This meant that each ruler would have a chance to control the entirety of Hell during their reign and fairly gather souls to appease the Deus Inferni. As previous over-harvesting had led to innocent humans being slaughtered as each realm struggled to collect souls. The harvesting that started the Great Plague.

However, the seven royals were not the most pleasant bunch of individuals. Their arrogance and twisted mentality were notorious, so much so that they were to remain holed up within their respective kingdoms, frozen in time awaiting their turn to rule as stipulated by the treaty.

The Wardens, relieved at the successful treaty negotiation, now had the opportunity to focus on their job of keeping rogue demons at bay. To ensure the smooth running of the agreement, the founding families of the Wardens dispersed to create strongholds all over the world, with the main one situated in Wales. Its close neighbour in England was led by Jaqueline Densbury, while the remaining three headed towards America and Europe, with the plan to expand and grow in due course. They took in orphans and abandoned children, moulding them into skilled soldiers to defend against the demons.

Jen Ward, who led the main stronghold, was warned of the impending danger that lurked in the shadows. The Wardens had to be ready for anything that would come their way as it was said, *'When she rises, Hell fire will surely follow…'*

The future was unsure, but one thing was for certain… they had to prepare for the worst.

Chapter One

Present Day

Kira's eyes fluttered open as she awoke in a cold sweat, her heart racing. For a moment, she was disoriented, unsure of where she was. Slowly, her surroundings came into focus. The soft morning light streaming through the pale lilac curtains in her room, casting a warm glow over everything.

It took a few moments for Kira's breathing to slow down, but eventually, she was able to relax. It had been the third time this week that she had woken up with a start, her mind racing from the recurring nightmare. She knew that she had to stop dwelling on it, brushing it off as just a nasty dream, but she couldn't seem to shake the feeling that it was much more than that.

Each time she had dreamt that she was in a dark room. A faint glow illuminated an ornate box in the centre of the room. Her heart pounding as she could hear clawing at the door to the room. The clawing grew louder followed by snarling. The door burst open, and something leapt at her, its claws and teeth sinking into her flesh. She knew it was just a nightmare, but the scratching and biting felt so real that her skin ached when she awoke.

With a sigh, Kira sat up and stretched her arms above her head. She knew that she couldn't stay in bed all day, no matter how tempting it seemed. Her shoulder-length midnight black hair sticking to the sweat on her forehead. The remnants of her mascara, smudged around her eyes. She was naturally beautiful or at least that's what her boyfriend told her, which may have been true if the apparent panda eyes were non-existent.

She hopped out of bed and couldn't help sucking in a deep breath when her feet hit the cold wooden floor, as she navigated herself to the bathroom. She didn't have time for a shower so she had to pray that the washcloth would work its magic. Grabbing it, she ran it under the tap, the cool water soaking into the fabric and started to scrub at her face trying to rid it of any remaining remnants of makeup that dared stay on her face.

She scanned through her wardrobe to look for appropriate work attire. It was a warm day and the lecture halls could be stuffy at times, so she picked out a simple black knee-length dress and paired it with black ankle boots.

Finally, washed and clothed, she sat at her dressing table and worked on fixing her hair for the day ahead. She had decided that today she would wear it half up, to hide her unwashed hair and secured in place with a Celtic knot style barrette. Kira descended the flight of stairs that separated her from the kitchen and proceeded to pour herself a cup of hot coffee, the liquid steaming, thick and black, adding a splash of milk to make it a drinkable temperature, she waited for the toaster. Coffee downed and toast devoured, she grabbed her bag and headed out of the house, locking the door behind her.

Kira looked at the scene before her, it was the same as always. Rows of houses, little cottages and gardens of wildflowers and greenery, but there was something missing, she couldn't quite put her finger on it and then she realised. The birds who were usually singing their sweet high-pitched tunes were deathly quiet. In fact, there was not a single bird in sight. Kira scratched her head, *peculiar.*

However, what did catch Kira's eye was an eerie looking man whom, was leaning against a tree on the opposite side of the road to where Kira was standing. She was sure that he was watching her. His eyes reflecting the sunlight, like pools of spilt petrol casting rainbows through them. Her eyes were fixated on him. The more she stared, the more intense the feeling of being watched grew, as if the man was looking directly back at her. It was the unnerving sense of being watched that caused her body to shiver and the hairs to stand on end.

The horn of a passing car released her from the trance, and she shook herself before continuing to walk to her car, which was only a few steps away. As she climbed into her car, she continued to glance back at the tree where the man was, to find that he had gone.

Click! Her seatbelt went into the slot, and she started the ignition. Pulling out of the drive she adjusted her rear-view mirror and her eyes opened wide. The man which had reappeared, was now following her, seeming to move lop-sided as she drove down the road. She put her foot on the accelerator and put enough distance between them both that he disappeared from view.

She had arrived at college, collected her class list and was sat at her desk awaiting the students for the first lecture of the day. As the eager students piled into the lecture room awaiting the start of this morning's seminar, the alarm on Kira's phone went off. *Here's to the start of yet another day*, she thought sarcastically as she flicked onto the first lecture slide. It wasn't the fact that she hated her job as it was quite the opposite in the sense that she loved her job. But lately, something had been niggling at the back of her mind and she couldn't put her finger on what it was.

Taking a deep breath, she sighed. Exhaling all of the air in her lungs, she imagined herself releasing the metaphorical raven which had been clouding her thoughts. And on with the lecture…

'Quiet down guys. Quiet! The bell will dismiss you all in a few minutes, but I just wanted to point out that the question for the assignment is; What makes people commit crimes? You can all go in any direction that you feel will make a compelling argument. Try to cover a few ideas from the opposing side and then conclude as to why you think people commit crimes.' The bell sounds off in the distance, followed by doors slamming and lockers opening, 'Okay everyone, have fun in Mr. Cole's lecture this afternoon and have a nice weekend.'

The rest of the day was a blur and not before long, Kira was sat down at her desk, her mind in deep concentration as she marked papers. She found her mind wandering again as she tried to work out what was so strange about this morning's encounter. *Surely things like that happen? He could have just been walking in the same direction that I was driving. He didn't actually DO anything to me..*

Her phone started to buzz, and it vibrated across her desk. Snapped back to reality, she turned the phone over to see who was calling her. *CRAP!*

The caller ID read 'Leon' and she instantly knew what he was calling about. She couldn't believe it was seven already! Her mind had been so all over the place that she had completely forgotten.

'I'm on my way as we speak' she answered as he questioned where she was. 'No, no I didn't forget. Got to go can't phone and drive.'

She hung up, tossed her phone into her bag and headed to the parking lot. It was their anniversary today, six whole years of being together, and whilst they lived together, Leon had been working away a lot, so it would be the first time she had seen him in three weeks.

She loved Leon, he made her feel safe and she didn't need to worry about things because he always took care of them for her. She found her mind trailing as she mulled over if there was a possibility, he would ask her to marry him. She knew years ago that they were end-game but he never seemed to want to let things go further. She found herself parked up outside of the restaurant, unsure how she got there and wondering if she had sped on the way whilst in autopilot. It was a restaurant that they had frequently gone to, nothing overly special but it provided a nice casual dining experience.

Leon was handsome, his eyes a vivid oceanic blue, contrasted against his platinum blonde hair. His devilishly handsome looks were increased as soon as he smiled back at her. Leon had that mesmerising and infectious smile that Kira just couldn't resist. He was leaning on the bar. Despite being late, his demeanour was oddly happy. Not that of someone who had been kept waiting, which was strange because he **hated** lateness. Kira had once arrived home late due to traffic and an unfortunate last-minute meeting at work, Leon had thrown her tea in the bin and refused to speak to her for the rest of the evening. That's how seriously he took not being late.

Leon took her hand, 'You have kept me waiting a long time…' Kira was about to apologise when Leon brushed a finger over her lips… 'not just tonight,' he smiled.
'I love you', she spoke as she kissed him, her lips softly brushing his.

Leon leaned back and laughed, 'Kira, I don't get it. I honestly don't. Before I met you, I lived without you and now. Now, I can't imagine my life without you.' He reached into his pocket with his other hand and brought out a tiny black box.

Leon paused and knelt down, 'I was going to wait until we were sat down enjoying our meal, but I can't wait another minute. I could spin off a whole speech about what you mean to me and how god damn special you are. But the truth is, is that I can't imagine my life without you. I know I have said it before but it's true. So, will you do me the greatest honour and promise to be in my life forever? What I'm asking is, Kira will you marry me??'

Leon popped open the black box, sat on the red satin cushion inside of the box was a ring, the epitome of perfect. It had a round diamond sat in the centre of the ring surrounded by smaller diamonds creating an outer ring 'halo' around the larger diamond, finished off with more small diamonds that encrusted the band. It glittered excessively under the restaurant lights.

She hesitated before replying, 'no.'

Leon choked on air when he heard her reply, 'What?'

Kira stood defiantly, trying her best not to smirk, 'I said no.'

'What- Why?' Leon looked defeated. He started to put the box away in his pocket.

'I'm joking! Of course, I will marry you. Always and forever, remember?'

Leon stood up and she flung herself at him, grabbing her by the waist he spun her around in the air. It was a picture-perfect moment. When he placed her back on the ground, he removed the ring from the cushion and slid it onto her ring finger, kissing her hand before releasing it. Leon smiled, the sort of smile that made his eyebrow raise in a flirtatious way, which also brought a smile to Kira's face. Leon spoke, in a husky tone, 'Are you ready to go for dinner?'

'We're here aren't we?' asked Kira, confused by his question.

Leon smirked, held the restaurant door open for her and ushered her through. Then he grabbed her arm and directed her towards the South carpark, 'This way milady.'

It was true that he was a complete gentleman and that he knew how to treat a lady, but Kira did not expect such a grand gesture, certainly not after the ring, which she spun around her finger, admiring its beauty. Outside of the South entrance, in front of the couple, was a sleek black limousine, 'Is this for us?' asked Kira as she could not believe what she was seeing.

'Only the best', he grabbed a hold of the door handle and gestured with his right arm for her to climb in. When they were both seated, he nodded to the driver, and they pulled off. Kira couldn't help the smile that escaped her lips. She had known him for years. Just when she thought she knew all of his tricks, somehow, he still manages, even now, to surprise her.

The limo made several turns and came to a halt. Leon frowned, raised a single eyebrow and then smirked. It was what Kira defined as a sexy, smouldering look and boy, did he pull it off! Leon turned to face her and whispered, 'today is all about surprises.'

Whilst Kira was puzzled as to what he meant by 'all about surprises', he jumped out of the limo and ran around to the trunk and began heaving several bags onto a trolley along with the help of the limo driver. Several thuds later, he poked his head around the door and exclaimed, 'Come on! We're going to be late!'

Leon pulled her out of the limo and allowed her to adjust her outfit accordingly. Then he began to tap his blazer pockets, first slowly and then frantically.

'What's wrong?' she quizzed.

'I. I. I need to go home; I've left something important.'

'Do you want me to come with you?'

'No. No, it's fine. I won't be long, but just in case...' Leon handed her an envelope, she lifted open the flap and pulled out a ticket, 'I don't understand? We can't just leave work and disappear?'

'It's all sorted. I sneakily booked a holiday for us. You said you wanted a spontaneous wedding, well here you go.'

'Oh my! But what about the family? Our friends??'

'All taken care of, we will have a wedding when we get back too'

'Two weddings, isn't that greedy?'

'Haha. Look, I really must get going or you will be going to our wedding on your own.'

'I love you,' she shouted as he clambered into the limo and pulled off. Leon wound down the window and blew her a kiss. After the limo had gone from sight, she headed inside, the clouds gathering for what appeared to be the start of a terrific storm.

Kira waited for what seemed like forever and the plane had started to board passengers. After deliberating in her mind, she decided it would be sensible to head towards the boarding area and wait for him there. That way they'd be closer to the plane if they had to board last minute. Kira had left him three missed phone calls and a bunch of voicemails. She checked the time; he had been gone for over an hour and a half. *What was taking so long?* Her mind started to wander. She had checked in and as far as the airport were concerned, she was to be on that plane. The choice; to go or not to go, was hers.

What if he had cold feet? I mean sure, he had arranged it all, but everyone can get cold feet before their big day. What if that's why he is taking so long….

They had gone through a lot together; numerous jobs, promotions and holidays. He had even met her adoptive parents. She had never met his parent's, but he had explained that they travelled a lot for work, and it was a rarity that he would see them. They had bought a little house together and everything was just so perfect. They had their own routines when they were both home and everything ran like clockwork.

Her mind had drifted off and the only thing which had jarred her back to reality was the fact that her phone was ringing in her hand. It was Leon. She had never been nervous about answering his calls but on this occasion, she had the unnerving sense that something was wrong. *Why else would he be ringing instead of being at her side boarding the plane?*

Hesitant she answered, 'Leon?'

'No, Ma'am this is Police Officer Braven.' Kira couldn't help herself when she heard the words 'Police Officer', knowing that he wasn't driving, made her all the more scared. All of which sent her into a state of panic,

'Oh my god, oh my god...this can't be happening. What's going on? What's happened?? Is he okay?'

'Ma'am. I would prefer for you to come down to the station or if you tell me where you are, I will send a police officer to come and collect you.'

'No! No! No! You will tell me now; I need to know what is going on!'

The Officer continued to insist that she would be better off coming down to the station, 'Ma'am this is not something I wish to discuss on the phone. The only reason I called was to get in touch and you are listed as the emergency number in his phone, we need to confirm that you are Miss Kira Darkthorn.'

'Tell me. Please. If you don't tell me, I am going to be panicking even more whilst waiting for the officer than I am now. Please, I can confirm I am Kira Darkthorn.'

Her voice sounded so desperate, the Officer's heart strings were pulled, 'Ma'am I am afraid that there has been a terrible accident...'

Kira was in a state of shock as she tried to process the information from the police officer. The rest of what he was saying was lost on her as her mind was consumed by the gravity of the situation.

Her chest tightening, it felt as if an entire building had collapsed on top of her. She struggled to take a deep breath, her heart racing with panic and fear. The Officer's voice became a distant murmur as she tried to grasp the reality of the situation.

Kira's mind continued to race as she tried to come to terms with what had just happened. She was overwhelmed with emotions and struggled to keep them in check. It was as if her world had turned upside down, and she was left feeling lost and alone.

Chapter Two

Kira found that her breathing had become extremely difficult and that her legs could no longer hold her body weight, and in one swift movement, she fell to the floor. 'Are you okay?' a voice asked as a hand tapped her shoulder. Straining to see, as her eyes were stinging from the salty water that they produced, Kira nodded. She tried to do her best 'I'm okay' response but the attendant who had asked her, was unconvinced however the attendant also recognised that she just wanted to be left alone and so the attendant nodded before walking away, leaving Kira on the floor, her back leaning on the wall of the departure tunnel.

She couldn't face flying to the destination her dead-fiancé had booked for them, nor could she face calling people to tell them what had happened. She couldn't face anything or anyone.

As the storm approached the airport, the sky gradually turned grey, indicating that it was going to pour heavily anytime soon. The atmosphere became gloomy, and the air around began to feel thick. Gradually, the first few drops of rain began to fall, hitting the roof of the airport and making a soft sound. But within minutes, the light rain turned into a heavy downpour. The sound of the rain thrashing against the glass windows of the tunnel grew louder, almost rattling them. Soon, the raindrops on the windows of the tunnel merged into a translucent sheet of water, blurring anyone's vision who tried to look out. The storm had finally arrived, bringing with it the promise of a cold, wet evening.

The final call for the flight had been made and Kira remained sat in the tunnel. She only moved when a flight attendant came to move her for safety reasons. Even then, she only made it a few yards before settling on an airport bench.

A young boy just a few seats down from Kira, started jumping up and down with excitement and began to call out, 'Ooo Lightning...Mum, Mum! Look Mum! Lightning!'

'Okay Sweetie,' the mother replied as she continued to drink her coffee. In the distance a siren was going off, the terminal mostly unaware and undeterred by it. Within seconds the once distant sound became an ear deafening screech as the tannoys announced,

'This is not a drill. Please can everyone move away from any windows and vacate terminal three. I repeat, this is not a drill, please can everyone move away from any windows and vacate terminal three immediately. I am sorry to say that we have been informed that flight 643 has exploded within minutes of take-off and that we should expect debris to fall. Therefore, I urge everyone to vacate terminal three at once and take shelter under the ticket office which has been made to withstand any impact.'

A deathly shiver took over Kira's body as she looked at the ticket in her hand. It read, Flight 643; departing at terminal 3, Seat 7b. *I was supposed to be on that flight. So was Leon, but he...I should have been in the limo, but he told me that I couldn't go with him. It's all my fault and now, everyone's dead.*

When she had followed the orders that everyone had been given, the group of people that huddled under the ticket area began to scour for any stragglers that may have not gotten the memo or had blindly chosen to ignore it. In the far corner of terminal three was a couple, who must have been in their mid-thirties, standing at the window watching whatever was happening outside.

Kira called for them to take shelter as it was dangerous standing there, but they didn't answer. Instead, they turned their heads incredibly slowly, and glared at her. She was used to being glared at, for many people have been glared at, at least once in their lives but it was the eyes that struck her. Instead of a standard eye colour, the couple's eyes were completely red. Flame red. She called for them again, maybe they hadn't heard her the first time and they turned to see if they had been called for? Maybe her mind was playing tricks and the *red eyes* were the funky contact lenses people wear nowadays?

Still, she knew that they were risking their lives lingering at the window. A flash of bright light blew the glass out of the terminal's windows, sending shards everywhere along with parts of the terminals walls that had been damaged by the blast. The debris from the explosion crashed onto the ticket booth, chunks of wood and rock scattering across the floor.

Kira's sense of reasoning had officially kicked in. Every time she called out for the couple, they just turned, glared and looked back at the window. It seemed as if they were waiting for something. That was when she first heard it, the crack of the ceiling above the ticket booth, the ceiling was going to collapse. The booth could not withstand another hit of debris, she screamed at the top of her lungs, 'The ceiling is going to collapse on us! We need to get out of the ticket booth now!'

Panic stricken customers began to clamber over one another to vacate the booth as soon as possible, while a group of customers and attendees began to call out to those in a panic, that it is safer under the booth as it is made to withstand such things. A second crack began from the opposite end, as another piece of the plane fell from the sky. Kira made a dash for the booth to try and grab some of those who had chosen to stay under there as the third and fourth crack occurred. Flung by the sheer impact of the collapse, she was sent hurtling across the terminal floor and landed with a thud. Pain rose up her body and everything throbbed with a red, rawness to it.

Her head, dazed from the incredible whack on the floor, made any images received through her eyes, hazy. She raised her head slightly and looked around, trying to piece together what had happened. Everyone was bloody and from what she could tell, no one had survived the collapse…except for the strange couple who were now advancing towards the pile of people strewn on the floor of the airport. Like ravens, they huddled around their prey with slightly cocked heads and hunched backs.

The male snarled and the female nodded in response, then they each pulled out an ornate blade. They waved the blades around, their actions fluid-like and in turn, they each touched the forehead of one of the bodies, from which a black shadow spilled out. The shadow, resembling an oil spill, shone with rainbows of varying colours as it slowly moved from side to side, the male stepped on it and sliced the shadow, severing whatever had been keeping it from floating off. Reacting like a helium balloon, it bolted upright but was captured when the male held up a red pendant, this action alone caused the shadow to stop in its tracks and it was absorbed into the pendant. One by one they continued this strange ritual until the pendant had devoured all of the shadows.

The couple stared straight at Kira as she tried to crawl away from them. Her head may be dazed but she was not stupid, and she was not going to fall prey to these two. 'What do you want me to do with her?' the male asked as he pointed towards Kira.

'We need as many as we can get. She's easy pickings.'

'Allow me to do the honour?'

'Of course, Brother.'

'You know. That's why I love you.'

As a predator would stalk its prey, he advanced in a slow manner. Apparently liking the fact, he was taking his time, his sister was grinning menacingly from behind him. Kira's heart began to beat wildly, any louder and she would be sure that someone other than her would be able to hear it. He turned his dagger so that it would be the perfect angle to kill her and raised it above his head, both hands clasping the handle. She raised her hand in a futile attempt to save herself as it drew closer, the dagger crashing down on her.

She was showered with blood, which sprayed everywhere. Kira clutched to where she thought she was bleeding from. *Well, that's weird. Either I'm dead or I am numb, because I can't feel a thing.* She sat up and examined herself. Yes, she was covered in blood and yet she was not injured from the dagger, she looked up and saw the male which had been holding the dagger above his head was now kneeling. His mouth spurting out blood, apparently choking on it. Kira squinted, *What in the world?* She thought to herself as she scrambled up from the floor, almost wobbling over as she tried not to step on any of the bodies that carpeted near where she stood. She covered her mouth with her hand as she examined the situation. The female was lay on the floor, keeled over with blood spilling out, unmoving. The male, who had moments ago tried to kill her, was also on the floor but he was still moving, convulsing as he choked on his own blood.

The adrenaline rush from the near-death experience was beginning to wear off and she was about to make the loudest scream of horror, in the history of mankind. Her body tensed up, preparing itself for this release of emotion but just before it could escape, it was plugged shut by a hand which was now on top of her own, covering her mouth.

The voice that spoke was one of authority, but she could sense that it had a gentle side to it, 'Shh, whatever you do. Do not scream. Okay?' She nodded her compliance to the voice's request. Her intuition had never failed her before now, so why not trust what it was telling her. That she could trust whoever this was.

'I am going to remove my hand now.'
When the grip on her mouth had been released, Kira sighed. Words failed her and she could not think of anything to say. Her brain however, was on overdrive. *What am I going to do? What do I tell people?? How can I explain what happened when even I don't know what happened?*
Her mouth finally knew what to do, 'What the hell happened here?'
'It's difficult to explain.'
'Then do try explaining, because quite frankly, I'm having difficulty understanding the situation. As to me, it looks like you murdered those two, and that guy tried to kill me.'
'Did you really think that through? Like you said, I killed those two because the guy was trying to kill you and the female ordered him to do it. You were in danger; it was merely self-defence. Sort of. He attacked you.'
'Oh. Well, that. That is reasonable. But that doesn't explain the fact that they had red eyes,' he cut her off mid-sentence, 'A plane in the sky had just exploded, it was probably a reflection of the fire or something, maybe even contact lenses. I can assure you that they do not have red eyes…naturally anyway.'
Defiant as ever, she was not willing to accept that what had happened was a

completely normal scenario, 'Well what about the fact that they were harvesting shadows.'

He uttered, 'I'm sorry?'

Kira realised that this was not the 'I'm sorry' it happened. But that it was an 'I'm sorry' of complete and utter shock. She decided that it would be best to elaborate for him.

'Yes. They were collecting shadows or something. All I know is that one of them touched the forehead of one of the, I'm going to call them victims. One of them touched the head of the victim and a shadow thing spilled out of them, they cut the shadow and it floated. Before it could float off like a balloon in the air, they captured it with a pendant.' Kira put her hands to her head. Hearing herself say it out loud, she realised just how delusional it sounded.

He turned to face where he had killed them, he bent down next to the male and yanked off what was hanging around the male's neck. 'Was it this, by any chance?' he enquired as the red pendant swung back and forth. Kira raised her head and lowered her hands from her face.

'Yes. It glowed a vibrant red colour when it sucked the things in. It's a lot duller now.'

'I see.'

'Well, I don't see. What were those shadow things? Who were they?' she pointed over to the couple.

'Look it's difficult to explain.'

'You've already said that. You haven't answered any of my questions. You keep deflecting them.'

'Ask me a simple question then', she was opening her mouth to speak when he continued to talk, 'and not about any of this.' He gestured his arms around him.

'Okay. Name. What is your name?'

'Luke.'

'Who are you?'

'It's difficult to explain. And before you say it- I am not deflecting either. It's true that it would be and is difficult to explain.'

'Fine, may I see your face?'

'Of course.'

He turned to face her and lowered his jacket hood and scarf that shielded his face from her.

'Oh my!'

'What-What's wrong??'

'You.'

Chapter Three

'What about me?'

'Leon, you look just like Leon. Your surname is Ward isn't it.'

'Everyone says the same thing, personally I don't see the resemblance. But then again, we are- Wait! How do you *know* Leon?' He emphasised on the 'know' and his eyes began to glare at her. Kira paused, *Is this a trap?*

It was true that the family resemblance was there especially with facial structure but there were a few differences. Whilst Leons eyes were blue and his hair platinum blonde, Luke's were a grey-blue and his hair was mousey brown.

Kira couldn't get over how similar he looked, 'I was his fiancée'

'His fiancée? Since when?'

'Since this evening, when he proposed to me. But then he…' Her voice trailed off as she began to sob, tears trickling down her cheeks.

'But then he?'

'He got in the limo and', sniffing up to avoid her nose running she wiped her eyes with the back of her hand, 'He's dead. He died in a car crash, he went home to get something and he never came back.'

Luke was furious, *How could this have happened?*

He didn't want to believe her, he wanted to forget that she had suggested such a thing. 'No! No! How do you know this? He might have gotten lost! It doesn't mean he's dead if he doesn't come back!'

'The Police informed me. They wanted me to go down to the station and speak to them.'

'Then that's what we have to do. We will go and by doing so, confirm that it is him.'

A rustling sound appeared, seeming to grow louder with every passing moment. Luke tucked away the pendant, 'We have to leave.'

'But what about the Police, the bodies?'

'Look, they've probably sent a dozen of Wrathlings after these two. Things like this-with multiple deaths, are usually done in packs. I only saw two, but from the rustling, I'm assuming that the others have finished harvesting with the deaths from the aeroplane and have come to check on things here. We're not safe.'

'Wrathlings?'

'Yes, that's what we call them.'

'We?'

'Look, there is a time and a place to explain things. This is not one of them. Now, my brother obviously loved you very much, the fact that he wished to marry you tells me that. Now if he really is dead, then I am not about to let you die on my watch. RUN!'

She turned to see the cause of all the rustling and was faced with around seven of the red-eyed humans. Red eyed **Wrathlings**. She corrected herself. Each of them had a red pendant swinging from their necks, some suspended on black cord and others on a bronze looking chain.

She ran. She ran as fast as her legs would carry her and then some. The airport had been apparently cleared from all people, possibly for safety reasons whilst the emergency services tried to push through to clear up the debris. But for now, it appeared that they were not coming anywhere near the airport in case any more of the debris fell from the sky.

They made several sharp turns through various doors, and then they came to a door that was locked. Panicked and tired from the running, the pair of them were panting.

Luke commented, 'This is the back exit. I parked my car on this side. If we could just.'
Luke tried to ram the door, but it wouldn't budge.
The rustling followed them. Unsuccessful at getting the door to open, he breathlessly said, 'We will have to find another exit.'

Luke ran back out, fearing that if they did not move, they would soon be cornered in this 'L' shaped bend. Confronted by the seven Wrathlings which were advancing on them, he ran back to Kira. 'Kira. New plan, we won't have time to find a new exit. Can you pick a lock?'
'Yes, but I don't know if I can pick this lock!'
'Try.'
'Well, why can't you try? It's your idea. I've never done this before. I've only ever seen it done in movies!'
'Have you ever killed a Wrathling?'
'No, what does that have to do with this?'
'Exactly.'

Kira sighed as she removed a hair grip from her hair and bent it into shape. She began fiddling with the lock, as Luke watched out for the Wrathlings. The first click came with ease.

'Hurry! They're coming!!'

'I'm trying! I never said I was an expert!'

'Let's not fight. Let me know when you've unlocked it.'

Luke removed the dagger from his jacket and swung it into a defence stance.

'Second click achieved.'

'How many more to go?' Luke changed his stance as the first of the Wrathlings had reached them. Kira glanced over to Luke and saw that he was both graceful and deadly with a weapon as he made a swift movement and the first Wrathling fell to the ground, howling in agony.

Luke glared at Kira, which caused her to continue working on the lock, 'I think that it is a three-click lock. I honestly don't have a clue' she yelled back at him. She continued to flick the grip in the lock, wiggling it and twisting as she tried to make the last click drop.

'Three!!!'

Luke ran towards her, as she pulled the door open. The six remaining Wrathlings hot on their tails. When they had managed to get through the door, Kira and Luke pushed it shut behind them. Luke spat out, 'Find something to barricade the door' as he fought to keep the door closed as the Wrathlings were trying to gain entry.

Kira came across a collapsible stool, 'Will this do?'

'Not really, but it should buy us some time to get to the car.'

She handed him the stool and he fixed it into a position which should hold the door closed. The pair located the stairs and headed down to the back parking lot. A loud crash followed after they reached the second set of stairs, smoke began to pour into the room.

Kira and Luke found themselves caught in a thick cloud of smoke that seemed to follow them, growing thicker as it drew nearer. As they breathed in the toxic fumes, Kira began to choke, feeling her head grow dizzy as the smoke inundated her senses. She grew increasingly uneasy as she began to suspect that the substance choking her was more than just ordinary smoke. Suddenly, she couldn't take it anymore and fell to the ground, clutching her head in pain. Luke, equally affected by the smog, coughed uncontrollably, but quickly regained his senses and lifted Kira.

Without losing any more time, he dashed toward the nearest fire exit door and pulled it open, leading them both to the sanctuary of the outdoors.

Kira began to stir. She could feel that something was holding her. The grip on her, tightened. She could feel the muscles wrapped around her, the scent of cologne washing over her. That was when it all came flooding back, *The Wrathlings!* She flipped that much that she nearly fell out of his arms. 'Kira, look. Will you stop wriggling!'

She turned her head to face him, 'Ow, my head.'

'I'm not surprised your head hurts. You took quite a fall.'

Kira looked at him and squinted, 'What was that back there? The smoke.'

Luke frowned and scrunched up his face, 'I honestly don't know.'

They found Luke's car and headed towards it. It was a black Audi TT hard-top convertible with red leather seats and a private registration plate. Kira admired the car, 'You have a nice taste in cars.'

Luke smirked, 'Well, I am glad that you think so. Otherwise, I'd have to make you walk there.'

She smiled at his response, he was nice, and she would have been proud to have him as her brother-in-law, but as fate would have it, it was not to be. He put her feet on the ground, slowly lowering her so that she would be steady and opened the passenger door for her. Kira thanked him and buckled herself into the car. Luke shortly followed suit. He sat himself in the driver's seat, buckled up and started the ignition.

'Ready?' he asked as he backed the car up, out of the driving lot.

She shrugged, 'I honestly don't know'.

They drove for around an hour and arrived at the Police Station.

'We're here' Luke announced as he pulled up into a space outside the precinct. Kira glared at him and warningly she spoke, 'Don't remind me'.

The pair hesitated outside of the car for a moment or two before deciding to venture into the station, *would they really want to know what happened?*

Kira grabbed Luke's hand and squeezed, *I'm scared to find out what happened to him, I can't imagine what Luke's going through right now.* Luke looked down at her hand holding his, whether or not it was more reassuring for her or for him, he was unsure but all he did know was this- he needed it.

Luke had resented his older brother for silly sibling things, but he never dreamed that his brother would die. Sure, he knew that it was inevitable, but he always assumed that Leon would rule first, marry the girl and have a family and yet his brother never got to do any of the above. He wasn't even sure how to take the news that he's gone or even how to break the news to their parents.

An Officer at the front desk asked them if they needed any help and as soon as they mentioned why they were there, they were ushered into a small room with two couches. Luke and Kira remained seated for five minutes before the officer arrived, apparently the officer was on his lunch break, to which he apologised for making them wait so long.

The Officer then went on to explain what had happened.

'We received a call about a loud crash involving a limousine and a lorry. When officers arrived on the scene the limo was engulfed in flames that the firemen were putting out, we haven't called you to ID the body as I am afraid to tell you that the body cannot be identified through recognition. We have used DNA testing to confirm his identity and the limo drivers. We found you through the contacts listed under his name, you are listed as his next of kin as his wife, yet there is no marriage certificate. Can you confirm this?'

'I am afraid that I am not his wife, we were due to get married that day but…' she couldn't stop herself from being overwhelmed with emotion nor could she stop the torrential downpour that was occurring from her eyes.

The Officer scratched his head, 'Oh, I see. As you are not legally his next of kin, I am unable to disclose any further information.'

'What??!!??' Kira couldn't decide whether or not she had shouted that out loud or whether it was an exclamation of shock, either way she could not believe her ears.

Luke wrapped his arm around Kira's shoulders, 'Well I am his brother, Luke Ward. So, you may continue.'

The Officer grinded his teeth at the fact he was granted permission to continue by a boy who looked about twenty, 'Oh. I am so sorry! Mr Ward. However, this is convenient that you happen to be his brother. I will have to confirm your identity before speaking about the case.'

'How many of you are working on the case?'

'I cannot disclose that information, but I assure you that we are doing the best that we can.'

Luke's face grew red with fury, it wouldn't have been as bad if the officer had handled the situation better but the fact that he was so blunt with Kira, having been the one to call her earlier and deliver the news over the phone but now all of a sudden it's a problem to disclose information to her.

'That's not what I asked. I said, how MANY of you are working my brother's case??' 'Mr Ward, calm down.'

His response flipped Luke over the edge. Luke shot up to a standing position, 'You don't have the right to tell me to calm down! I lost my brother, and she lost her fiancé, yet you have the audacity to tell me to calm down? Instead of avoiding my questions and giving me blanket answers, you could just tell me- How many officers are working my brother's case? Since, Officer Braven you thought it fit to deliver the news of his death over the phone.'

The officer huffed at him and he knew that he would not win against Luke, especially given that he broke protocol earlier by revealing information over the phone, so he gave as little to him as possible, 'Two officers, alongside the staff in the lab.'

Luke kept his tone noticeably short, so that each and every word came out as if it had been spat, 'Two? And what are they doing right now??'

The Officer grunted at Luke's firing of questions. So much so, that his words were very much matter of fact, 'Sir, they are filling in paperwork about the accident. It's a report that everyone must complete after an accident.'

It appeared that Luke was getting angrier each time the officer spoke to him and Kira knew that this wasn't going to end well, she shook her head as Luke's mouth continued to open, 'So you mean to tell me that instead of finding out what the HELL happened to my brother, your two officers are filling in a report? How is that going to solve it?'

'Mr Ward. I am going to have to ask you to leave', the officer scrunched up his face.

Luke's questioning was going nowhere, and he wasn't going to get the answers he wanted. Kira intervened, 'Luke, come on. The officer is clearly going to be no help.'

Luke's arm was grabbed by Kira who guided him out of the small room, into the lobby and outside to the car. As the door was closing, the officer stared at them leaving. His eyes reflecting on the glass of the door, a brilliant red.

Chapter Four

Luke was furious, 'Why did you tell me to leave? We could have had answers!'

Kira understood how he must have been feeling, she too was angry at the way things had gone just now but she knew that agreeing with him would be an unwise decision, 'Luke, he wasn't going to give us anything. Let alone answers. The Police aren't going to help us.'

'Then, that's it then. Unless-', he cut off and began pacing back and forth, lost in his thoughts. Kira tilted her head in bewilderment and wondered as to what he meant, 'unless what?'

Luke fished out his keys from his pocket, found the car, unlocked it and replied, 'Unless we go and do some digging.'

'What are you expecting to find?'

'Something, anything. If he is really dead then there has to be a body, if there isn't then he isn't dead.'

'They already said that the body is unrecognisable.'

Luke opened her door for her, as he leaned to close the door, he whispered, 'But is there a body?' Luke climbed into the driver's side and closed his door.

'Why do I get the feeling that you are about to suggest something that is illegal?' asked Kira, as she fastened up her seatbelt.

Luke replied in a 'matter of fact' fashion, 'it is only illegal if you get caught. And I for one, do not wish to get caught.'

'I'm really not sure about this', Kira had never done anything like what was to come, her mind was telling her to get out of the car whilst she still could, but her heart was telling her that she needed to know. Luke grabbed her hand and squeezed, as if he knew exactly what her heart was trying to tell her, 'Answers. We need answers.'

Kira began tapping her fingers on the passenger-side window, 'I'm nervous. What if there is a body? What if there isn't?'

Luke pulled the car over and turned to face her, 'I don't know the answers to the questions of *what if*, but what I do know is this; I am here for you no matter what happens.'

Kira half-smiled, she was happy that she was not alone to deal with this, and then it came crashing down on her. 'I'm being so inconsiderate, here you are having lost your brother and I'm the one complaining about how nervous I am. This must be heart-wrenching for you.'

'Kira. Listen to me. It's okay, we all have our own ways of dealing with things, mine starts with finding out what happened to my brother.' Luke pulled back out and drove off, heading north.

'I don't want to bother you again, but I just have a question, which morgue are we going to?'

'Oh. I didn't even think about that. How many are there?'

'One covers the, erm, the North and East I think. The other covers the South and West. So, I am going to say two.'

'Is that your final answer?' asked Luke, imitating a gameshow host.

Kira rolled her eyes, 'Yes.'

'Now we just have to work out which one my brothers possibly in.'

'We could try phoning. If we don't get an answer then we are back where we started.'

'Right, there's a phone book in the glove compartment.'

Kira fumbled in the glove box and retrieved an old phone book, the pages curled from age and moisture.

'M…Motor repairs, MOT centres, Morgues.' She grabbed her phone from her back pocket and began dialling the number listed,

'Hello? Hi, Yes. I have an odd request really, I'm looking for a body. The person was in a car crash earlier today, might be under the name Ward? Oh, I see. No that's fine. Thank you very much for your help. Goodbye.'

Luke glanced over at her and then turned back to face the road, 'Any luck?'

'No, but that means he has to be at the other morgue. Which according to the address listed in the phone book, is about a ten-minute drive from here, we just need to turn left at the next intersection.'

'Right' replied Luke who focussed on driving and not missing the intersection turning. He had just turned when Kira alarmingly yelled, 'Luke, we have company.'

Her sentence just finishing as the car jerked forward from a hit to the rear of the car.

'Damn! Since when did Wrathlings get so clever?'

Kira choked, 'Wait- What? You mean to tell me that the things trying to run us off the road are the same as the ones at the airport??'

'Unfortunately, yes.'

The car jerked forwards a second time and then a third. Kira began to panic, 'Hurry, speed up. They're far too close for comfort.'

'Tell me about it.'

'They're not going to stop until they run us off of the road.'

Luke's eyes lit up like a lightbulb moment, 'That actually might not be a bad idea.'

Kira's jaw dropped, 'You have got to be kidding me?' She turned to look out of the back window.

'Brace yourself, on the next hit. I am going to flip the car.'

The car behind them included four Wrathlings which Luke had counted just before the final hit. He spun the wheel hard which resulted in the car flipping over, the wheels still spinning from the impact.

'Kira? Are you okay?'

'Well, honestly I have been better.'

'Talking's a good sign though. I need you to pull down the sun visor on your side. Inside is a cloth which houses a blade. Be careful as it is sharp.'

She moved the sun visor and a clothed item slid from it; it slid down the windscreen. Kira grabbed it and passed it to Luke who was bracing himself as he unclipped his seatbelt resulting in a thud as he hit the windscreen and dashboard.

'I'm going to have a look around. Unclip yourself and stay near the car,' ordered Luke.

'Luke. Don't go out there.'

'I'll be fine', Luke turned and was faced with a Wrathling who had a scar that ran vertically down the centre of his face. The Wrathling lunged at Luke with a curved blade which looked as if it was made by a badly skilled blacksmith, the metal rippled with kinks and bubbles.

Luke finally managed to get the upper hand and stabbed his dagger through the neck of the Wrathling, blood pooling on the floor as the body dropped to the ground. The second Wrathling flung herself onto Luke, sending him flying backwards, she bared her teeth which had been filed into points, her eyes glowing a brilliant red. Her teeth sank into Luke's throat as they wrestled on the floor. The unexpected attack had caused the dagger to slip from Luke's grip and was caught by the female Wrathling, who growled; 'To die by one's own weapon, the irony. Clearly the Wardens aren't all they have made themselves out to be. Prepare to meet the King'.

The Wrathling fell to the side of Luke with a thump. 'Not today Satan,' said Kira who was holding a blooded rock. She threw the rock to the side of the road, her hands shaking as she offered them to Luke to help him back to his feet.

Luke tried to lighten the situation and ease Kira, 'You'd think that if they really wanted to kill you, maybe they should do less talking?'

The other two Wrathlings had scarpered, but the fight had left Luke with some war wounds. Bruised ribs, a few grazes, and a major gash to his neck where the female Wrathling had sunk her sharpened teeth into his neck. Luckily for Luke, the major artery had been missed. Still Kira was unimpressed with his current presentation and demanded that he take her to the local pharmacy where they could get supplies so that she could use her basic first aid skills, which all teachers were required to have, and attempt to patch him up.

'I really don't think that that is necessary Kira', Luke groaned as his right hand clung to his ribs.

'And I don't think you are in a position to argue with me. You can't exactly protect me in the state that you are in which is what you promised to do back at the airport so, which is it? You allow me to take you to the pharmacy willingly or you fight me on this, and I still take you to the pharmacy. One of the options is easy and the other one, well I can make the entire trip miserable', Kira stood tapping her foot awaiting Luke's decision.

'As much as I would like to see how you would make the trip to the pharmacy miserable, I also don't want to. Although I hate to admit it, I could really do with some paracetamol.'
'Well, that settles it.'

Kira pulled out her phone which thankfully survived the whole ordeal and began to search for the closest pharmacy to their location. Which luckily was only a twenty-minute walk away since they had no car.

Begrudgingly Luke followed Kira as her phone led the way to the local pharmacy. The twenty-minute walk went by in complete silence as neither Kira nor Luke had the energy to hold a conversation. What would they even discuss? Near death experiences?

Kira wanted to know more about the world that these Wrathlings come from, but she knew that it would take longer than they had the time for, and Luke didn't look like he was in the mood to discuss his life history, his brother's history and the Wrathlings.

If anything, Luke looked like he was going to drop to the ground imminently. Kira briefly closed her eyes as she let her skin bask in the warmth of the sun as they trudged to the pharmacy. In that brief moment, as she had suspected, Luke fell.

Kira just about managed to catch his arm to stop him from completely hitting the deck. Although, this required great strength as Kira was not physically strong and Luke had a lot of muscle mass. Still, she managed to drag him the last ten yards into the pharmacy.

Once in the pharmacy, the Pharmacist rushed over to aid Kira, who was now stumbling under the weight of Luke. He was an elderly looking gentleman however despite the aged appearance he was very spritely and took Luke from Kira, aiding him into a nearby chair, with extraordinarily little effort.

Kira looked at the gentleman who was wearing a bronzed name tag that read, *Mr. Chimico.*

'What's wrong with him?' Chimico exclaimed.

'We…' Kira thought quickly about what she could say and also, what would be believed. *Attacked by paranormal entities* would probably get her locked up.

Kira blurted out, 'We were in a car accident' as she had become aware that he was raising his eyebrows awaiting the rest of her initial response. 'He's got quite a few cuts and bruises but not enough for the emergency department. So, we just need some bandages and such.'

Mr. Chimico seemed otherwise unconvinced that the injuries were unworthy of an emergency department. But he was also old enough to know when to stay out of such things. 'Personally, I think he needs looking over by medical professionals however I cannot force you both to go to a hospital. So, I will recommend you both to go, especially after a car accident. But I will also help you get the items you need to patch him up.'

'Thank you', replied Kira who was now suffering from fatigue.

After a quick rummage of the shelves, they had gathered the necessary supplies and when Luke had regained enough strength. Kira helped Luke into the nearby bathroom and then aided him in cleaning the wounds with sterilising alcohol and then bandaged up the open flesh. Kira offered Luke the paracetamol she had also grabbed off of the shelves however Luke refused it.

'On second thought, I don't think paracetamol will make much of a difference here.' Luke removed his hands from the sides of the sink and stumbled slightly. Kira rushed to his side. 'I will be fine Kira,' he groaned.

Kira rolled her eyes, 'You're as stubborn as your brother you are.'

'Speaking of my brother. We have wasted enough time on me. Let's get going.'

Kira bit her lip and frowned, 'Only one slight problem there. We've still got quite a way to go before we reach the morgue, with this little detour, and we don't have any form of travel.'

'I can sort that out' he replied.

Luke wandered over towards the pharmacist and called out, 'Mr. Chimico.'

Mr. Chimico turned around, 'How can I help?'

Luke placed a hand on the top of Mr. Chimico's head.

'We need your vehicle. So, if you could take us to it and give us the keys, that would be great.' Luke removed his hand. Mr. Chimico paused, smiled and then responded with, 'of course, follow me.'

Kira looked confused. *How had he managed that?*

As the duo followed Mr. Chimico to his car, Kira asked Luke, 'How did you do that? How did you convince him to give *you* his car? Are you like, a vampire? Can you compel people to do what you want?'

Luke laughed, not a small laugh but a big belly reaching laugh. 'No Kira, I am not like a vampire. You watch far too much TV. They also base all of that vampire nonsense off our abilities. We don't call it compulsion but more along the lines of suggestion.'

'But it's the same thing?'

Luke rolled his eyes and sighed, 'I suppose so.'

Keys handed over, Mr. Chimico waved them goodbye, and the duo set off to the morgue.

Chapter Five

A few detours later, due to Kira being somewhat geographically challenged, the duo arrived at the morgue. Luke used his powers of suggestion to convince the receptionist to let them through to the back. Once in the back, the duo ran into the autopsy technician who was not at all happy at the pair's presence.

'What are you two doing back here?' She demanded.

Luke thought fast on his feet, hoping to hide who they truly were in case of another run in with the Wrathlings; 'We were sent back here to view one of the bodies for a case we are working on.'

The Technician spoke, still visibly angry, 'Well, who sent you?'

Luke replied coolly, 'Senior Officer Jenkins Ma'am'

The Technician looked taken aback as if the name held a lot of weight behind it, 'Oh, very well then.'

The morgue was lit with bright LED lights and the air was cool, the ventilation systems keeping the area cold to aid the preservation of the bodies when out of their respective drawers. Kira had never been into a morgue and after today's trip, she was sure that she would never want to walk into one again.

Luke maintained his fake persona of authority as he brought up his brother's name. 'We are here to see the body of a Mr. Leon Ward'.

The Autopsy Technician headed over to one of the drawers, 'Yes of course. You may want to place some cotton wool in your nose or use some of the menthol ointment around the edges of your nostrils. This one isn't pleasant smelling'. She gestured towards the metal tray sitting on the trolley. Kira was frozen in place, unable to move an inch let alone head over to the tray. Luke maintained his place next to her.

Kira was not unfamiliar with death. She had lost several family members in her lifetime, but she did not expect to lose the man she loved this quickly. She was not prepared for this. She would never have been prepared for this. A lump had formed in her throat.

The Technician opened the drawer and pulled out the tray which housed the body draped in a white cloth. She gently pulled the cloth back. Kira's eyes widened as they took in the sight before her. She keeled over and began to wretch and heave, before collapsing to the ground clutching at her chest and stomach. Her heart shattered after seeing Leon's body, or what was left of his body.

The woman was right. The body smelt horrendously as it was charred black. Leon's distinguishing features long gone as they had perished in flames. The sight was worse than Kira could ever have imagined and now it was permanently etched into her mind. Luke was leaning down, his mouth moving but Kira couldn't hear any of the words coming out of it. He tried to put a comforting hand on her shoulder, but she shrugged it off. The thought of having to talk to anyone or be near anyone at this moment in time was just too much to bear. She got up off of the cold, hard laminate floor and ran straight out of the room, through the reception and into the parking lot, where she held her head in her hands. Unsure where to go or what to do next. Tears streaming across her flushed cheeks. She wasn't sure if she was angry or upset, possibly even both.

She forced herself to sit down on the curb before she did something stupid. Something reckless.

Luke eventually emerged from the morgue and headed towards Kira. His face solemn on his approach.

Luke's voice on the brink of breaking as he spoke, 'I'm sorry you're upset but I want you to know Kira, that I understand.'

Kira's face flushed even further. A deep scarlet red. Her eyes glaring as she focused solely on Luke's face. Her voice venomous as she spoke. 'How can YOU possibly understand how I feel?'

She got up from the curb and stood directly in front of Luke, 'How can YOU possibly understand?' She pushed Luke with both hands, her fury growing, 'Leon was MY fiancé. The love of MY life. A man I wanted to spend the rest of my days with, grow old with and start a family with. So, you say you understand but how could you even remotely understand how I feel? Simply put you can't and don't. Because not only did I lose the man I loved. A man I thought I knew. I have also lost the memories I had with him because as it turned out I didn't actually know him at all. He chose to keep his entire life, his entire identity a secret from *me.'*

Kira continued to push Luke again and again. Pushing him back towards the building's wall. Luke's back firmly pressed against the abrasive bricks. His voice had dropped so it was so soft it was almost a whisper, his face full of sadness, 'Kira.'

Kira paused from pushing him and the tears returned as if a giant flood gate had opened and the once flushed cheeks had all of the colour drained from them. She wobbled forward as if the weight of everything had caused her to overbalance. Luke reached out and steadied her before pulling her close to him. Holding her in a bear hug until she had calmed enough for Luke to discuss their next move.

After a few minutes, her breathing had calmed and the colour had slowly begun to return to her skin. Her eyes widened at the realization that she had completely lost it and took it all out on Luke.

'Luke I…' before she could finish Luke had placed his hand over Kira's mouth. His eyes on alert. Moments later, he gently removed his hand.

'We need to find cover. It isn't safe here,' he whispered.

Kira lowered her voice, 'Is it Wrathlings?'

Luke swallowed, 'I don't know but I do know we are being watched. I can feel it.'

He guided Kira back to the car.

Luke helped Kira into the car and closed the door behind her, 'We need to lay low. So, I think we should find somewhere to stay for the night.'

Kira was feeling tired after the days drama so it sounded like the perfect suggestion, 'I could do with a few hours to recharge.'

'Okay. That settles it. I will find us a little motel.'

Luke began driving, they passed a few motels, one had no vacancy and the others looked beyond run down. Fifteen minutes later they arrived at a little motel with quaint, little flower-pots outside the main reception.

Luke jumped out of the car, 'You stay in the car and I will get us a room.'

Kira waited in the car. Her eyes exhausted from all of the tears that she shed and sights that she had seen. She let out a small yawn and her eyes became heavy. She struggled to keep them open, awaiting Luke's return. She closed her eyes for a brief moment, hoping a short rest would help them feel less heavy. When she opened her eyes after the brief amount of time, she was surprised to find herself lay on a bed in a motel room. Her shoes at the side of the bed.

Kira cocked her head, 'Did you?'

'Did I carry you to the room? Yes. You were asleep in the car and after the events you have experienced. I thought the least I could do was allow you the sleep you clearly needed. I just wasn't expecting the sleep to be five minutes long.'

'I've only been asleep for five minutes?'

Luke laughed. 'Yep, conveniently you wake up after I lug you to the room, took your shoes off and put you on the bed. If you didn't want to walk to the room, you could have just said.'

Kira's belly grumbled. She couldn't even remember when she last ate something. 'Luke, do you want to grab some food? I could eat a horse.'

Luke frowned, 'Please tell me you won't actually eat a horse.'

'It's a phrase. But I am starving.'

'I will order a takeaway to the front desk and collect it under our pseudonym. What do you want to eat?'

Kira paused before replying, 'anything, you choose.'

'You're the one that's hungry. I was giving you the choice. Let's order a pizza. What toppings do you have?'

'I, um, I will share whatever you order.'

'Kira. Genuine question. Why are you making me decide what we are having?'

'Well. Leon used to just order everything for me. I never had to choose or decide.'

'So, you never got a say?'

'It wasn't like that before you insinuate anything. He just knew that I didn't like deciding thing's, so he did it to be kind.'

'Okay. I will let you have that. Food picking can be hard. What about your favourite colour?'

'Green.'

'Leon's favourite. Favourite band?'

'Fall Out Boy.'

'Again, Leon's favourite. Favourite flower?'

'I don't have one. I can't stand the smell of them.'

Luke's brows furrowed, 'Exactly what Leon would say. Kira, did you ever get a say in the relationship with my brother?'

'Leon liked making all of the decisions and helping me to choose clothes and such. I liked not having to decide.'

Luke's eyebrows furrowed further, 'and you truly believe that?'

'I. Well, he never asked me for my views on things, but I know that he was just being kind and helpful.'

Luke kept his answer short this time, 'I see.'

He didn't want to probe any further. He knew his brother could be controlling at times. Leon was the same when it came to being a Warden. Leon wanted to be involved in everything and even tried to argue with the Elders when he was refused control over certain political areas. Yet Luke didn't expect Leon to try to control someone that he was supposed to have loved.

Luke asked, 'Well, let's do things differently. What pizza do you fancy trying Kira?'

Kira paused, took the phone off of him that housed the takeaway menu and she read the options. The BBQ chicken option sounded nice. But she really liked the sound of the BBQ Hawaiian. *But would Luke like pineapple on his pizza?*

Kira hesitantly asked, 'How about the BBQ Hawaiian?'

'Sounds perfect Kira. Do you like garlic bread?'

'I do.'

'Great that settles it then. I will place the order and collect it when they phone to say its near.'

Kira relaxed back onto the bed and Luke paced the room. The room wasn't very big, but it did house two single beds and a very clean bathroom.

Luke announced, 'I'm going to grab a shower before the takeaway arrives. I don't need to raise any more eyebrows. The motel manager has already looked at me funny once.'

He proceeded to undo his shirt and place it onto the little stool that made up for the lack of a chair in the small room. His back was full of abrasive marks and scratched as if it has been rubbed against something hard. Kira's eyes widened as she realised that she was the cause of the injuries to his back.

Kira stood up, 'Did I do that? Outside of the morgue?'

'Kira it's fine honestly. It just looks worse.'

Kira closed the distance between her and Luke. Her fingers tracing the marks on his skin. When she stroked over a few of them, he winced.

'I'm sorry Luke.' Her fingers continued to trace his skin when she came across an unusual scar mark on his back. When she touched it, he turned to face her grabbing her hand.

'That is the mark of the Wardens. It's a branding given to the Warden men.'

'Only to the men?'

'The women are given a different marking. Each sex has a different role to play. Women are more strategic and planners. The male Wardens carry out the plans that the women have strategised. But they are also our second line of defence for ground zero. Highly trained with exceptional weaponry. Whereas I'm more the hand-to-hand combat with a knife occasionally thrown in.'

'Is it quite lonely? You talk a lot about defence and chaos but not about any relationships or friendships.'

Luke's eyes became sad, 'Who would want to drag someone into a world of fighting and potential danger?'

Kira covered her mouth, 'I didn't mean to pry.'

Luke's eyes met Kira's as he moved her hand away from her mouth. Kira leaned towards Luke. He felt like a magnet pulling her towards him. Her lips brushed his and her right hand reached up to caress his cheek. Luke grabbed her hand and stepped back.

'Kira, I don't think we should.'

Kira spun round and ran to the bathroom, shutting the door behind her. She slid down behind the door and hugged her knees. She had crossed a major boundary. *But why did it feel so right? It felt like she had known Luke for her entire life. Of course, it did! He was Leon's brother! They would have similarities!*

Luke called through that he was going to the main reception to collect the takeaway and would be back shortly. Luke put his badly stained shirt back on and closed the door to the room making sure that the catch secured it. He punched the motel wall on his way to the reception.

He had stopped her from kissing him but that was all that he wanted. He wanted her. He needed her. But he had to stop her, so that she didn't regret anything. She had just lost his brother. He had just lost his brother. It was all kinds of messed up, but she was perfectly imperfect and he had developed strong feelings for her.

At first, he brushed them off as feelings for a person you would treat as a sister but then he soon realised that these were more than that. They were feelings that he shouldn't have. Kira was his brother's fiancée. But the feelings were there all the same.

He made it to the main reception and collected the takeaway before heading back to the room. His mind still reeling. Where did these feelings come from? They hadn't known each other for long but there was something deep inside of him that ached for her.

Kira was now sat on her bed. Her face flat. He hated seeing her like this. He wondered if he could have handled the encounter better. If he had hurt her by reacting the way he did.

'I have the takeaway,' announced Luke, as he set the food down on the stool. Kira tucked into the food, its warmth filling her angry, rumbling belly. Nothing more was discussed that night. The food was devoured, and the pair went to sleep on their single, lumpy motel beds.

The sun arose and glared through the thin, almost transparent motel curtains. It was time that they made tracks. The pair left the room and dropped the keys off with little to no words exchanged between them.

Chapter Six

As soon as the car doors were shut, Luke set off driving, leaving Kira to question where they were going.

Luke glanced at Kira, 'You're wondering where we are going aren't you?'

'As a matter of fact, yes I am. Where are we going?'

Luke smiled; it was a half-hearted smile but a smile, nonetheless. The tension between them eased. 'We are going to the Keeper of Records'

'The Keeper of Records?' questioned Kira.

'The Keeper of Records for the Wardens and the Seven Levels of Sin.'

'Wow.'

'Well, you said you wanted to know and for me to explain things, so I figured that you might as well meet the single most knowledgeable person that there is for our realm.'

Kira smiled, 'Thank you.'

'You're welcome and I will try to explain things but feel free to follow anything and everything up with the main man himself.'

Kira adjusted her position and prepared herself for the knowledge that was coming her way. There was no going back now.

Luke started, 'So, as you could have guessed from the name there are indeed seven levels of sin. One for each of the Seven Deadly Sins. Now obviously each King or Queen sin cannot rule at the same time. It would be and has been chaos. So, a treaty was created and every seven years they alternate. Each one ruling for that time and then on to the next. Wrathlings belong to the King of Wrath and shouldn't be randomly collecting souls as they please, so something has gone wrong. Now, I am a Warden. I come from a family of Wardens. My brother, your fiancé was one too. We manage what is known as Ground Zero of Hell. We help to keep the peace. Manage the seven-year rotation and kill off any rogue demons who aren't behaving or aren't hibernating if it isn't their levels turn.'

Kira gasped, her brain trying to absorb the abundance of information Luke had just thrown at her, 'Wow that's a lot. So, you don't live here? Like up here?'
Luke raised an eyebrow, 'I live in Hell.'

Luke pulled the car to halt. 'We have arrived.'

The home of the Keeper of Records was nothing like Kira could have imagined. It was an abandoned little shack of a house with boards instead of windows and tape labelling it as condemned. The front garden, or what used to be the front garden, was filled with overgrown weeds, shrubbery and bits of rubble, and fallen roof tiles. The place was a disaster zone and Kira was certain that the person they were looking for must have been long gone as no one could live in this mess.

Kira put her hand to the side of her head and scratched, 'Luke, are you sure that the Keeper of Records lives here?'
Luke laughed, 'Well, where else would he be?'

Kira raised her eyebrows and Luke realised she didn't understand that his comment was a joke. She had much to learn.

'He lives here. It's just a front. If he didn't try to hide from the humans by making it look derelict. How many do you think would wander into something that looked like a bookstore with the number of records and books he has? Book-people are the most dangerous threat. Knowledge is power and they have it in abundance. Therefore, low key is always best,' laughed Luke as he moved some old boards.

Kira followed Luke inside, ducking under the boards that covered the front door. She muttered, 'low key is always best' under her breath and then gasped.

You know those scenes in movies? The ones where the main character is introduced to a giant library with a grandiose staircase and fine drapery. That was what Kira was looking at.

Her face a picture of amazement at the reams of beautifully bound books that filled the walls of the room that they had walked in to.

A room far from the low key that Luke had spoken about. Luke turned to face Kira and smiled as he watched her take in the view. He had to admit that it was pretty impressive, but he had been here many times and the initial astonishment of seeing this place had worn off. Still, he couldn't help but watch Kira's child-like wonder as she took in all of the room's offerings.

Luke called out into the seemingly empty room, 'Keeper?'

'Is that who I think it is?' A voice called back, the echo bouncing throughout the vast space.

'Depends on who you are expecting', answered Luke.

A figure appeared at the top of the central staircase and Kira's eyes widened. As he descended the staircase Kira observed the figure. He was pale. Almost translucent. With short, shaggy white hair and red deep-set eyes.

Kira nudged herself closer to Luke. The figure put her on edge and scared her a little. She kept imagining the Wrathlings and wondered what this figure was, because he was certainly not human.

'Luke Ward. It's been a while. I assume you're not here for a coffee and a catchup?'

'Unfortunately, Nathaniel not this time and you know I prefer a stronger drink.'

'Too bad. Just when I thought I had company.'

'Maybe next time. I'm on official business.'

'You're always on official business but you never seem to fill out the official record request forms. Maybe this time, you could make a special effort to fill them in before you leave.'

'I promise to go to the official form room before I leave.'

Nathaniel sighed, 'What can I do for you? And who is this lovely woman?'

Nathaniel took Kira's hand and leaned forward to kiss it, 'A pleasure to meet you Miss'. Kira shuddered.

Luke swallowed, 'Kira. This is Kira. She is, was, my brother's fiancée.'

Nathaniel straightened and took several steps back. His face reddening from embarassment. 'I'm sorry, I didn't mean to over-step Mr. Ward.'

Kira looked confused. Nathaniel genuinely seemed terrified after the reveal of who she was. *But he didn't do anything wrong did he?*

Luke shook his head, 'At ease Nathaniel. Those laws are so outdated anyway. I need you to keep Kira company whilst I go on the search for the records I need.'

'As you will. I will gladly keep our newest family member safe.'

Luke wandered off into the shelves of books and Kira was left alone with Nathaniel.

Nathaniel gestured for Kira to follow him as he walked off into a hidden corridor. Luke was long gone, absorbed by the books so she figured she might as well join Nathaniel. Luke seemed to trust him.

Nathaniel led her into a little, cosy living room. It housed two lilac, velvet loveseat sofas, a miniature coffee table and a huge, bronze ornamental fireplace. The fire was roaring with life and smelt of the most incredible burnt wood. The warmth instantly calmed her, and she sunk herself into one of the crushed velvet loveseats.

He cleared his throat and sat himself down on the other loveseat, 'I suppose you have a lot of questions for me.'

'Just a few. If you don't mind.'

'Fire away.'

'Why do all of the human history books talk about Lucifer being the King of Hell? AKA The Devil? Which is far from true if it's actually being run by the Seven Deadly Sins?'

'You can't believe everything you read. Humans are mainly simple creatures, and it was easier to tell them that there was only one king, the Devil that rules Hell. The place bad people go to. If you started to go into the nitty gritty of it all, you'd drive some humans mad.'

Kira nodded, it had been hard for her to try to come to terms with killer demons.

'But why Lucifer?' she asked.

'Well, that was a creation of the Wardens. They wanted to use the story as an example. To prove a point, that bad people get punished. In the case of Lucifer, he fell from Heaven and well, landed himself in Hell as punishment. The word Devil was used as an acronym amongst the Wardens, and it sort of filtered into the story as it spread over the centuries.'

'What did it stand for?'

'Don't Ever (be) Vile In Life'

'A fair acronym to live by. So, Lucifer never existed?'

'Well, that depends on who you ask and personally, I have never met a Lucifer... but I have only been alive for 2000 years so, who knows?'

He paused and scratched his head, 'Kira, would you like to view some of the records? You can have a look around. I need to catch-up with Luke.'

Kira nodded and started to wander, her fingers outstretched stroking the binds of antique leather-bound books, the literary bug inside of her could scream at having such an extensive collection at her disposal. One book in particular seemed to call out to her and she found herself drawn to it, as if the book itself had magnetic properties. Her skin tingling as she got closer to it and when she pulled the cloth book from its position on the shelf, she found herself staring at the sigil on the front, which was now glowing.

Kira rotated the book to look at the back, to see if it had batteries but to her surprise there was nothing. Nothing to suggest it even had any form of wiring that would allow the front to glow.

She turned it back; the glow was now pulsating as if it was breathing in and out. Changing from a dim light to a brilliant amber glow.

'Kira?'

Kira spun around and saw that both Luke and Nathaniel had entered the room. They were both wide eyed staring at the book in her hands. The pulsing glow was quickening. The book suddenly burst into flame and Kira dropped the book with a shriek. Luke rushed over to check Kira over and see if the flames had burned her skin.

To his surprise, her hands and arms were completely unscorched and unharmed. The book however was now a pile of ash, the metal sigil that adorned the front of the book was intact. Nathaniel fished it out from the ash and wiped it on his clothes. His head cocked to the side as he inspected it.

Nathaniel quizzed, 'Kira. Are you sure you knew nothing about all of this?'

'What? No, of course not.'

'I don't believe you. You're lying,' Nathaniel's face was twisting with anger as he put the sigil directly in front of her face. 'You see this? This is the sigil of the Wardens. To activate it, you have to be a supernatural entity'.

He thrust the sigil towards her and Luke, 'Now, you can understand why I don't believe you and why you are not welcome in my home. Leave. Now. I want no part in this. I want it acknowledged that I am not involved with the two of you.'

Luke stood in between Kira and Nathaniel, urging Nathaniel to calm down, that he was under no threat and that the Wardens would not inflict anything upon him for aiding the pair. Nathaniel waved his hands and both Luke and Kira were now stood outside. The derelict appearance in front of them once more.

Kira threw her hands up in the air. 'What the hell was he talking about? Supernatural entity? So, I'm supposed to believe that I am some kind of what? A Wrathling?'

'Not quite. There's a lot more supernatural beings in the world than you probably realise. Are you sure you don't know anything about any family links to the supernatural? Maybe a curious yet strange uncle?'

'Seriously Luke?'

'I'm trying to make light of a dark situation. Clearly, we don't know everything about you and Nathaniel seemed spooked enough to kick us out.'

'Well, what do we do now?'

'There isn't a 'we'. This isn't your fight. Nathaniel told me some pretty alarming things back there about how there's potential unrest going on in the Hells and there's only one place I can go that can hopefully shed some light on it.'

Kira folded her arms in defiance, 'Luke, we've been through a lot together and now you're telling me that I'm on the outs and you're going it alone? Seriously?'

'Kira don't.'

She raised her eyebrows and bit her lip, 'Don't what.'

'Don't press me on this.'

Luke's remarks did not deter her. Kira playfully frowned, 'Or else?'

He grasped her, one hand on her shoulder and the other entwined into her hair. 'Your defiance is infuriating yet I can't help but feel intoxicated by you. It's like you're a missing piece that I have been longing for, unaware that it was missing. And then to find out that you were betrothed to my brother. Makes this all so wrong. To feel this way. To know it's what I want. I yearn for you. I yearn for the taste of your lips. The touch of your skin. Your affection.'

'Luke I'

Luke drew back, moving away from her, 'I'm sorry Kira. I overstepped. Just forget I said anything. It can't happen. We can't happen.'

Kira brought his hand down from her hair to her cheek.

'Luke,' she whispered, as her eyes locked gaze with his. His eyes were full of longing. She couldn't help but feel the pull towards him. It was unexplainable. But her heart yearned for him too. *If only this wasn't so complicated.*

Kira released his hand and lowered her head. She felt ashamed for evening thinking about making moves with Luke when there was so much going on and they had both lost Leon. *Maybe the feelings were just grief.*

Luke grabbed her hand and led her around the back of the derelict building.

'What are we doing?' quizzed Kira.

'We are getting some plain old revenge. Nathaniel shouldn't have treated you like that and besides, we need a new set of wheels.'

Luke pulled off an old dust sheet exposing a prized, Harley Davidson.

'Wow. He's going to be mad if we take this.'

'Maybe, but he would have to find us first…'

Luke smirked and handed her a helmet.

'We've got somewhere to be, so we better make tracks now.'

Chapter Seven

Luke hopped onto the seat and helped Kira onto the bike behind him. Helmets secured, Kira wrapped her arms around Luke's waist and the duo set off.

The journey to the House of the Wardens was going to be a long one but the pair needed to make as much headway as possible in order to reduce any potential run ins with the Wrathlings.

Kira could feel the warmth of Luke radiating through her arms as he drove. She knew that they had a lot to discuss when this was all over but, as conflicting as the feelings were. She couldn't deny that they were there.

There was nothing else for her to do except mull over her thoughts whilst embarking on this journey. Her focus was broken when Luke slowed down to pull over to the side of a dirt track road.

Kira asked quizzically, 'What's going on? Are we being followed?' Her eyes widening as if startled awake.

'No, or at least I don't think so. But my eyes are growing weary, and we can't be at our best if we are tired and that's when mistakes could happen. So, I needed to pull over to get out the map that I stole from Nathaniel's archives.'

Luke rummaged through his pockets and fished out a folded sheet of paper. The page itself was blank. Not a single mark or drawing present. Kira wasn't quite sure how this was supposed to be a map given it had no instructions or diagrams. Although, with the constant information overload of things she didn't know existed, it honestly wouldn't surprise her if the map could talk or transform into some portal thingy.

Kira stared at the piece of paper with a fierce intensity, 'So… is it a magical portal?'

'No but it is magical. It's reactive paper, it will only reveal itself when blood from a warden touches it,' Luke pulled out a safety pin and pricked his finger.

Squeezing his finger to manipulate the blood into coming out, until a small droplet formed on the tip of his finger which he smeared it across the empty page.

The page sparked and caught aflame. A strange kind of fire that only scorched the paper and left Luke without a mark. The map was aged. What would have once been a crisp parchment map was now antiquated, the smooth paper now crumpled, the edges curling inwards. But still the wording was clear. 8 chunks of land divided with one connecting to another through a passageway.

Kira scanned the map, 'What do the names mean? Avaritia, Libidine, Invidentia, Segnitia, Gula, Fastus and Iracundia'

Luke without glancing at the map recited the translations for each in the order Kira had asked, 'Greed, Lust, Envy, Hell, Sloth, Gluttony, Pride, Wrath.'

'So, in other words, they named their kingdoms after themselves? Well, that's a bit egotistical.'

'Yeah, I think they thought naming them in Latin would cover up that fact but here we are.'

Kira rubbed her eyes, 'So, what does this map have to do with finding somewhere to crash for the night?'

'This? Absolutely nothing. However, the other side is what we will be using.'

Luke flipped the page over and on the back were coordinates glowing a brilliant violet. 'Put these into your phone's maps'.

Kira tapped away at her phone and waited for the destination to load. According to her phone's maps the location was actually just a place in a wooded area. Unless they were pitching a tent, which seemed unlikely given the lack of camping gear or lack of anything on their persons. She really hoped Luke had a plan as sleeping out in the open whilst other worldly creatures were out to kill them didn't make an ounce of sense.

Luke glanced at the phone and traced the route with his index finger. 'Shouldn't be too hard to get there. Should make it by dusk.'

They were back on the road a few moments later. Kira was amazed by Luke's memory as he didn't stop for directions. Taking each twist and turn of the route with ease. Then they were faced with a very bumpy terrain as they approached the wooded area. Luke turned off the engine and pulled over. They were going to have to make the rest of the journey on foot.

By this point Kira was exhausted and even though it had been days since her initial hit with the information overload and the devastation of her life going up in flames, it was feeling a little too much, a little too overwhelming.

Kira's mind wandered as they trekked the wooded landscape. She found herself deep in thought mulling over the events, her feelings for Luke and her feelings of loss for Leon. Her brain was frazzled and the more she pondered everything, the more she felt like she was drowning. It wasn't something she could share with Luke as he just wouldn't understand having lived his entire life in the supernatural world, but she hadn't. What Kira was going through wasn't just an everyday occurrence and she was struggling.

Luke could sense that something was going on with Kira and the feeling was eating away at him. *Afterall what did he expect? She had gone through so much in such a short space of time. I don't think anyone could go through so much trauma and not come out feeling ...off.*

Luke sighed and slowed his steps down until he came to a standstill. 'Kira?' his voice was soft as he spoke her name, an air of concern surrounding it. She turned, having realised she had sped ahead of him and stopped in her tracks. He continued, his voice calm and steady, 'Kira, do you want to talk about it?'

Kira's face sank. It wasn't the face of sadness or worry, but the face of someone who was trying to remain strong being called out on it.

'I wouldn't even know where to begin Luke, so it is pointless even trying.'

'Could you just entertain the idea that you can trust me with your thoughts? I will just listen, no judgements.'

'It's got nothing to do with trust or judgements. Just that I am not so sure that you will understand how I am feeling, how this all affects me.'

'I can only try Kira. At least let me try.'

Kira brushed loose hair away from her face and rubbed her cheeks.

'I don't think I can do this.'

Luke focussed in on her face, 'This?'

'All of this. The whole Seven Levels of Hell and Wrath- thingies and demons and wardens and no. It's just too much. How am I supposed to deal with all of this just being thrown at me. Not long ago I was excited at being engaged and having a semi- normal life. I feel like I am drowning. Trying to process all of this with no-one who really, truly understands what I have gone through is just.'

Kira slumped to the floor and cuddled her knees to her chest. Luke knelt beside her. His hand resting on her shoulder.

'Kira, you are right. I don't truly understand how you are feeling because I have grown up knowing all of this. Brought up in this world where I have knowledge of things you never even thought were real. It's a lot. The only thing I can relate to is the loss of my brother, your fiancé. But if it helps, I do know someone who might have more of an understanding about how you are feeling.'

Luke tucked her hair behind her ear. His face earnest with concern.
'You really think that this person will understand?'
'I know so.'
Kira jumped up with feigned enthusiasm.
'Well then what are we waiting for?'

Luke stood back up, straightened his clothes and they both continued their travels. As they continued to trek through the overgrown woods, the sky became overcast, the kind where a storm was clearly imminent. The first drops of rain tumbled to the ground and the temperature plummeted with the sudden change in weather.

Kira's skin started to cool dramatically, with the lack of weather appropriate clothing. She shivered. Luke noticed her shiver and with a helpful smile, he proclaimed that they had arrived at their destination.

Kira glared at him as if to say *'seriously*?' Which for any onlookers would be an accurate statement of fact. As the pair were just staring at a large part of an open field. An empty, large field.

Luke turned his hand palm up and made a small incision on his hand. He then turned his hand down and clenched it into a fist. Blood trickling from the fresh wound onto the ground below. A cloud of violet smoke started to rise from the ground and then a flash of lightning hit the exact spot where Luke's blood had landed, and a portal appeared. One of many portals to the stronghold. Luke took Kira's hand and guided her through the portal. It slowly closed behind them. Kira watched as the field faded away before turning back around.

Luke gulped before gesturing,

'Welcome to my home.'

Chapter Eight

The Warden Manor was as exquisite as Kira had suspected. It gave off an air of royalty as well as revealing a lengthy history. The manor was beautiful and ornate. Various stained-glass windows adorned the front with tall turrets and a flag flying in the wind. It was situated in an extensive courtyard with various trees growing and blooming. It reminded Kira of the stately homes you would see on tv, the ones often used for royal dramas.

The lawn was covered in sweet smelling blossoms of unusual colours. It was incredibly well maintained for the size of it and Kira wondered how they managed to look after such a large garden. Kira and Luke headed down the paved road to the manor's entrance.

The entrance was certainly not a let-down given its enormous pillars and stone statues depicting various animals. The eagle was Kira's favourite.

A tall woman, in her fifties, was waiting in the hall. When she saw the pair enter her face grew a large smile and she rushed over to Luke, embracing him in a hug.

'I am so glad you are home safely,' she said as she stepped out of the embrace.

Luke half-smiled and rubbed his brow, 'Me too, but there is something I have to tell you and father.'

Her face changed from joy to concern, 'He is in the library. You know how he is. Always studying.'

The three of them headed to the library which was even grander than Nathaniel's and if it was under different circumstances, Kira would have loved spending time in here reading.

Luke's Father was the double of his son, albeit older but you could certainly see the family resemblance. If not for the age you would have said Luke and his dad were twins. The same mousey-brown hair and the same blue-grey eyes. Whereas the platinum blonde hair came from their Mum. She stood at the side of Luke, her blue eyes gleaming with happiness at seeing one of her sons. She had the same hair and eyes as *Leon*. Kira's heart twinged at the thought of Leon. It had been a while since she had truly thought about him and now the sadness seeped back in.

Luke introduced Kira and in turn they told Kira to call them by their first names, Amira and Leopold. Then Luke lowered his head and told his parents what had happened and about all the attacks by the Wrathlings that they had encountered along the way. His Father was outraged, his Mother was distraught. Kira wanted to give them some space, so she wandered out into the hall and found herself staring at old paintings depicting various battles, celebratory scenes and one depicting the signing of what Kira assumed was the treaty between the seven kingdoms of Hell.

She continued to walk down the hall and admired each and every tapestry and painting along the way. Stopping at one which seemed to draw her in. She couldn't help but want to touch it.

She stroked the tapestry and thought it peculiar that such a secret had been contained for millennia. Suddenly, she was overcome with a wave of emotions and memories that were not her own.

Kira's eyes rolled backwards and she fell to the floor. Convulsing she started to mutter an incoherent language.

When she came to, the room had altered, and she was no longer stood with Luke and the other Wardens. Instead, she was in the grand hallway and could hear ceremonial music coming from one of the far rooms.

She was drawn to the music and felt herself pulled in its direction. As if the melodious music was enchanting her and controlling her. She found herself pushing open large, engraved wooden doors. Stepping into the room her attire changed and she was dressed in luxurious silk and velvet robes. The kind that would have been worn in the renaissance period.

Rows of unfamiliar faces turned to greet her and bowed their heads as a sign of respect. At the end of the room was a large throne. She was seated a few rows back from the throne but was close enough to admire its beauty. The carved details on its armrests, depicting a crow and a snake. The gilded feet that the throne rested upon.

Everyone rose as a figure emerged from the doorway. He walked the exact stretch of aisle that Kira had just traversed. Everyone repeated the bowing of the head as a mark of respect for this figure and he stepped up towards the throne and placed himself onto it.

The figure looked familiar, although Kira couldn't quite place why or where from. She could feel piercing eyes on her, and she met the figures gaze. When she focussed on his eyes she realised exactly where she knew this particular person from. One of the paintings. Albeit she wasn't quite sure that he counted as a person, but he certainly was the King of Wrath.

She looked closely at the people in the front row and there they all were. The other six sins. Lust, Gluttony, Greed, Sloth, Pride and Envy.
Wrath was approached by a figure dressed head to toe in a black cloak with black garments underneath. As if the person was impersonating a living zombie, the face gaunt and colourless as if they had been entombed for centuries and this was the first breath of air.

Wrath was handed objects that reminded Kira of crown jewels. The kind that she had seen on television when royals were crowned Kings and Queens, rulers of realms. First came a sceptre of gold which was embellished with emeralds of various greens. Then came an orb shaped jewel which glistened in the few streams of light that cut through gaps in the large tapestries and curtains that adorned the room.

The zombie looking man made Wrath repeat a statement about ruling Hell and embracing its people, its ways and the agreement that he would pass the throne to the next ruler in seven years from today. Wrath agreed and everyone stood up.

Next came the other six sins, who bowed their heads in front of the new ruler and placed six small boxes at his feet. According to the zombie it was a token gesture that each King and Queen would pledge allegiance to the current ruler of Hell and to abide by the accords that were in place regarding the seven-year rule.

Everyone then returned to their seats and Wrath stood up. Still holding the orb and sceptre he called out a name although it was too faint for Kira to make out, but she felt her body stand up and move towards him. She was certain he did not call out Kira but another name, still her body continued to walk towards the King.

The tapestries and curtains started to fade away and slowly the rows of guests and the six sins disappeared along with it. Then slowly the King of Wrath started to fade away too and she found herself stirring against cold stone.

'Kira are you alright?'

Luke sounded concerned. His eyes focussed heavily on her face. Kira felt lightheaded and shook her head repeatedly as if stirring from a bad dream.

'I just had the weirdest dream.'

Kira relayed everything she had seen and heard to Luke and the other Wardens. Amira's eyes grew wide.

'Not possible.' She exclaimed.

Luke cocked his head to the side. Amira spoke with a startled tone, 'She just described one of Wraths coronations with extreme detail.'

'So, it wasn't a dream?'

'I don't believe so. What you described has actually happened. I don't know how this came to you, but I do believe that what you actually experienced was a flashback of sorts.'

'I touched the tapestry and then that's all I remember before I had the dream. Or the not-a-dream.'

Luke bit his lip, 'But Mum, I thought flashbacks like that only happened if the person was alive at the time. It was supposed to be like a memory trigger or retrieval rather than a psychic experience.'

'I don't know Luke. I have never witnessed anything like it. Or know of anyone who has had a flashback. I don't think one has been recorded for centuries.'

Amira paused and pushed hair away from her face before continuing, 'I would have to do some more research before I could tell you anything. Leave it with me.'

There was a tremendous bang followed by roaring flames. Screams were heard from the far reaches of the manor and calls to action were initiated. Wardens appeared fully armed and ready for something... As Wrathlings piled in from every entrance and window.

'We're under attack' shouted one of the Wardens as the Wrathlings charged at them. Amira commanded Luke to get Kira to safety as she joined the other Wardens in battling against the Wrathlings. More and more Wardens came to the battle, but they were outnumbered against the countless Wrathlings who continued to enter the building.

Luke fought off a few Wrathlings as they took a staircase down into the catacombs of the manor. Kira was about to head to the right as Luke grabbed her arm harshly and directed her in the opposite direction. 'You DO NOT want to go that way.'

He grabbed a pre-lit torch off of one of the stone sconces and guided Kira down the tunnel. 'It should be straightforward down this tunnel and into the courtyard.'

Kira shook her head, 'You shouldn't have said that'.

'Why?'

'Because nothing is ever straightforward.'

They turned a few corners and continued further into the tunnel away from the commotion of the ongoing battle between the Wardens and the Wrathlings. Smoke started to filter into the tunnel from above. Luke handed Kira a strip of fabric to place over her nose and mouth as the smoke grew thicker.

Sweat droplets ran down Kira's face as the temperature increased. The stone walls were heating up and becoming hot to touch. Luke pushed on a thick wooden door. It refused to budge. An old, rusted lock was the culprit.

Luke started to frantically look around the tunnel. Waving the torch around as he did. The flame flickering with the violent waving. Luke tentatively touched the stone walls, trying to pry a rock free from the aged cement. His fingers singed from the hot stones. He managed to loosen a rock and freed it from the wall, it tumbled to the floor.

He tore another strip of fabric from his shirt and wrapped it around his left hand and the repeated it for his right hand. He grasped the rock firmly and bashed it a few times against the aged lock. The lock tumbled to the floor with a loud clang. Heavy footsteps echoed down the tunnel followed by distinct snarling.

Kira gasped, her voice muffled by the fabric she clutched to her face to limit the smoke, 'Wrathlings.'

'Let's not waste any time then shall we.'

Luke yanked Kira's arm and they headed up an old, iron rung ladder. Luke pushed hard against the circular grid and moved the cover from the hole, allowing them to both leave the tunnel. He quickly kicked it back into place and coughed a few times to clear his lungs and inhale the fresh courtyard air. He looked back at the Manor, which was now engulfed in roaring flames, smoke bellowing outwards.

They were far enough away from the manor that the thick smoke had not reached the far courtyard, but Luke's face looked like the air had been sucked straight out of him and he began to hyperventilate. Clutching at his stomach and bending over.

Kira rushed to his side and dragged him onto the grass verge so he could sit down. Kira placed herself in front of him.

'Luke,' she caught his gaze as his eyes flickered around, his breathing sharp and short. 'Luke, I need you to work with me. It isn't safe to stay here, we have to get moving but I need you to work with me first. Nod your head if you can do that.'

Luke slowly nodded his head. His face remaining colourless.

'Okay, good. Can you tell me where you are?'

'The….court….yard.'

'Good.'

'When is your birthday?'

'May…May 19th 1995'

'Okay, now I need you to breathe with me. Breathe in for five seconds and then out for five seconds. One….Two…'

Luke followed her voice, breathing in for five and out for five. His breathing slowly returned to normal, and colour began to flush his face.

Luke jumped up and stumbled a few paces before resuming his usual '*go-getter*' demeanour. A shout came from behind one of the courtyard trees, 'We've got some!'

Several Wrathlings appeared and started to charge at Luke and Kira. The pair picked up the heels and ran as fast as they could. At Luke's best strength he could have easily kicked some Wrathling ass but in his current state he didn't like his odds. Not to mention they were both weapon-less after fleeing the Manor.

Luke dragged Kira and headed directly towards a towering oak tree. Running at full speed directly at its trunk.

'Luke watch out.' Kira used her free arm to cover her face and eyes as she waited for the pain of running into a tree trunk to hit her. But it never came. She removed her make-shift arm shield from her face and was surprised to see two Jeep-looking vehicles.

Luke answered before she had even asked the question, 'Protection parameters. In case of an attack. I suppose being pre-emptive works occasionally.'

Luke grabbed a full satchel off a nearby shelf and tossed it into the first vehicle. He then placed his hand onto the vehicle's bonnet and the engine started up. 'It's keyless' he chuckled to himself. 'Hop in.'

They both bundled themselves into the car and Luke put his foot down on the gas. The vehicle accelerated with lightning quick speed and propelled them down the remainder of the courtyard with ease. The Wrathlings that had been chasing them were slowly disappearing out of view along with the burning remains of the Warden Manor and centuries, if not millennia's worth of history.

Chapter Nine

'What do we do now?'

Kira looked at Luke earnestly. They had both been through so much. They had both just watched Luke's home go up in flames.

'We return at nightfall.'

'What if the Wrathlings haven't left?'

'We're not going to the Manor, just one of the outhouses. There is a passageway in one that we are going to need.'

Luke's face was plastered with a look of determination mixed with rage. Luke was ready for a fight, which worried Kira because he had nothing to lose. His family and his home had been taken from him. *Luke had already shown that he had streaks of recklessness inside of him but what would a Luke without any restraint be like?*

They drove around until nightfall, making use of the vast land that surrounded the Manor. Whilst the house was situated within a large courtyard, outside of that was a vast open space full of grassland and trees.

'So, this is Hell?' asked Kira as they continued to drive around until it was time to return to the house.

'Part of. This is where the main stronghold is. Sat directly above the entrance to the seven kingdoms. The other strongholds are all earthside. Hidden in plain sight. This is the only one in the Hell realm. It's time to go.'

With the headlights off they parked up at the entrance to the courtyard and made their moves under the cover of darkness.

Luke had identified one lone Wrathling on the way to the outhouse and dispatched of it with ease. Careful not to make a sound when doing so.

The door to the outhouse creaked as it was pulled open. Luke grabbed old oil cans and paint cans off of the shelves. The writing on the labels were in another language. He began to pour their contents out onto the floor into the shape of a pentagram. When the pentagram was complete it started to produce an ebbing glow, which pulsated as if it was alive.

Luke turned and held his hand out towards Kira, 'Are you ready?' She took his hand and stepped into the circle of the pentagram. Kira took a sharp intake of breath as flames licked up around them. The flames completely encapsulated them and then the flames dissipated.

'So, this is Ground Zero?' said Kira sarcastically as she stared at the flashing neon sign that proclaimed, *Welcome to Ground Zero*. The room hosted various tapestries showing pivotal moments in the history of Hell. There was also a grand clock hanging from the ceiling. Its casing was ornate and inside it depicted who the current ruler of hell was by illuminating the kingdoms name. As expected, this was the Kingdom of Wrath.

Luke clenched his fists, 'It is. It's also the start of us going to the Kingdom of Wrath and the start of me getting revenge for my family.'

Kira touched his arm lightly and looked him in the eyes.

'I understand wanting to avenge your family and I want nothing more than the people who killed them to suffer but we are not prepared for this. We might as well just hand them our souls right now.'

A voice called out, 'Well, that would save us some trouble. Can we take you up on that offer?'

Kira and Luke spun round to face the speaker. It was the larger of three Wrathlings. These were unlike the others which had human appearances, but the eyes were distinct. All three were grotesque creatures. With arms as long as their legs and talon sharp claws. Their skin a tinged green and blue. None of them had any hair.

Kira trembled. Not only were they outnumbered by one, but they were also unarmed. *This was beyond reckless. We are going to die down here.*

Luke's eyes narrowed and his face was determined, 'Ah but where would the fun in that be? Don't you want to be able to brag that you bested a Warden? Rather than us just surrendering?'

The Wrathlings growled in agreement and charged at the pair. Luke and Kira ran in the opposite direction. Heading towards large oak doors. They quickly shut the doors behind them and looked for items to barricade it with. There was a large chunk of wood and some bricks. They wedged it shut but it wasn't going to hold for long. Kira looked at Luke with panic.

'Luke, we're trapped.'

'I know.' His feigned strength and fake determination had worn off and he was truly just as scared as Kira was.

The Wrathlings were hammering at the door. Occasionally a large bang occurred from them charging at it. The wood and bricks were slowly slipping. It would soon be over. Kira felt a warmth wash over her and a wave of confidence. She couldn't explain it but she was prepared for them to come.

The wood gave way and the door burst open. The Wrathlings quickly heading towards them at the far end of the room. There was no other way out. No windows to climb out of. Nothing.

The Wrathlings lunged at them, and Kira closed her eyes. She expected to feel pain and the fangs or teeth of at least one of the Wrathlings but instead she felt nothing. Nothing came. *Is this what death feels like?*

Kira's body began to shake. Well, someone was shaking her. She opened her eyes and found that she was still in the same room, and it was Luke that was shaking her, the Wrathlings were nowhere to be seen.

'Where did they go?' quizzed Kira as she looked for signs or traces of them.

Luke scratched his head, 'I don't know. They were here. They lunged at us and then there was this flash of light and then poof. They vanished. I have never seen anything like it.' He breathed a sigh of relief before announcing, 'Let's keep moving and get what we need'.

He started to head out of the doors, keeping watch for any more Wrathlings that may appear or attempt to ambush them.

Luke directed Kira to a vaulted room and picked up a small piece of stone. He used the stone to cut his hand and placed it on the vault door. Sparks illuminated in a circle around his hand and the vault door opened with a clang.

Warehouse style shelves lined the walls with rows and rows of weaponry. There were your typical weapons of guns, grenades, and swords but there were also weapons that Kira had never seen in her life.

Luke handed her some small daggers and a strap to attach them to her waist as well as an ornate sword. Luke loaded himself up with weapons of various sizes and shapes, before announcing their departure from the vault.

Luke lead Kira down more winding corridors and straight to a stone archway that led into a large circular room with seven more arched doors. Each door with a different glowing symbol.

In between each door was a fabric flag with emblems and a word. Avaritia, Libidine, Invidentia, Segnitia, Gula, Fastus and Iracundia. The seven kingdoms of Hell.

'Luke, why is this Ground Zero if its seven kingdoms?'

'Seven levels. Each kingdom is connected by a staircase of bones. Wrath is the first and then you descend further into hell as you travel to each kingdom. These doors are merely a shortcut to each kingdom. Ground Zero is managed by Wardens so we basically keep things in check. There shouldn't be any Wrathlings at ground level. Only royalty and Wardens are allowed. So, something has really gone awry.' Luke tentatively looked around.

'Oh lovely. A staircase of bones. Wait?! Have we got to travel down one of those now?' Kira's voice becoming more exasperated as she spoke.

'Did you want a rainbow and a unicorn?' Luke laughed and shrugged his shoulders.

Kira smirked, 'I guess I don't really know what I expected but I didn't expect to be travelling on a staircase made out of bones. But it is Hell I guess so…I don't know.'

They headed to the door of Wraths kingdom and Luke pushed it open. Kira hoovered. Her fingers had started to tingle, a sensation of warmth travelling through them, and they started to glow with a strange red tinge. As quickly as they started to glow, they stopped. Kira shook her head and brushed it aside and prepared for their descent down the staircase of bones.

The staircase was horrifying. Skulls intertwined with cement and other skeletal remains. Kira could have sworn that she heard a distinct crunch when she stepped down. She started to heave and had to calm herself down.

Luke was several steps ahead and turned to ask if she was okay. Kira assured him that she was fine and put on her best brave face to support her statement.

He turned back around and continued to descend the staircase. When they reached the bottom of the stairs, they were standing in the middle of a scorched field. Bodies were strewn across it as if it was the aftermath of war.

'You shouldn't be down here,' boomed a voice from across the field. It lurked in the shadowy reaches. Just out of sight but the eyes glowed a brilliant red. It moved silently towards them. When the figure was close enough and it was clear that it was just another Wrathling, Luke spoke up.

'Well, we wouldn't need to be down here if your King was more approachable and kept you lot in line.'

It growled back venomously, 'How dare you speak of the King like that! You will regret those words you, worthless bag of flesh.'

Luke half-smirked, 'Worthless bag of flesh. I'll take that, I have been called worse.' Luke floored the Wrathling and held a knife to its throat. 'Now, if you would be so kind as to take me to your King.'

The Wrathling scoffed, 'He isn't even here. The King left the kingdom ages ago. Something I can say isn't likely to happen for you.'

The Wrathling wriggled and then began to combust before completely disintegrating into ash. From across the field there were dozens if not more of Wrathlings and all of their red eyes were focused on Kira and Luke.

'Run,' whispered Luke and they shot back up the staircase. The Wrathlings followed suit and began to chase the pair.

He slammed the door to the kingdom shut and poured blue tinted powder across the seal. The powder caused the door to become a block of thick ice.

Luke proclaimed, 'That should buy us some time.'

Once the pair had stopped to catch a breath they realised that they could smell smoke. They followed the smoke all the way to the start of Ground Zero. The flags and emblems that were hung in the circular room were all piled up in the centre and were burning ferociously.

The 'clock' which once depicted which level of Hell was the current ruler had been destroyed, tapestries depicting peace, unity and the signing of the hell treaty have been scorched. Luke took in the sight, 'This isn't rogues. Something is truly wrong with Hell.'

Wardens were rushing around attempting to put out the flames and some started to head down the corridors in an attempt to assess the damage. Luke was surprised to see so many Wardens.

Chapter Ten

A man who oozed authority called out, 'Luke! What a pleasure to see you alive!'

The man was in his mid to late sixties, with a full head of silver hair. His arms held behind his back as he stood in a relaxed stance. Luke did a double take, 'Adrastus, it can't be'

Adrastus stroked his stubbled chin, 'Long time. Just a shame it's under such circumstances.'

'Couldn't agree more. I'm assuming they called in quite the calvary? Is Nira along for this one?'

Adrastus shook his head, 'Nira is currently hunting lower demons who seem to think they can call the shots in the streets of Italy.'

'She sure keeps busy from the bits of news that filters back to the stronghold.'

'She does. But I'm afraid I don't really have time for a catchup. I have to organise the clean up crew and then take over as temporary acting head of what's left of the main stronghold. Only the East wing survived. I have organized Lieutenant Caiden to escort you to an armoured vehicle where you will be taken to our Warden safehouse. You will need to be processed and it'll take some time, but hopefully not too long Luke and we can have you scouting out and hunting Wrathlings.'

Adrastus gestured for the Lieutenant to approach them.

'Lieutenant Caiden, please escort Luke and this young woman to the safehouse. They have been requested by the council for questioning.'

Caiden ushered them out of Ground Zero, opening a locked metal door that revealed a marble staircase. They exited the staircase through a large metal grid. Once the grids lid was secured back into place it vanished, leaving no trace that it ever existed. Kira was amazed, although she was sure that she had much to learn and that for Wardens, things like this were just everyday occurrences.

Caiden opened the door to the back of the vehicle and instructed Kira and Luke to get inside. His voice husky and harsh, how Kira imagined prisoners were spoken to. The door was slammed behind them, and Caiden got in the front passenger. The driver already inside.

The journey to the safehouse seemed to take what felt like hours and Kira was becoming restless. *Shouldn't we be out there …helping? What did Adrastus mean by the council wanting them to be questioned anyway?*

Luke held her hand which seemed to settle her nerves. As long as they were together, they could handle whatever came their way and she felt safer with Luke around, should any Wrathlings appear.

When they arrived at the safehouse, which looked more like a normal cottage than anything special. Two teams were waiting for them. A team of female wardens escorted Kira to the left and a team of male wardens escorted Luke to the right, leading them both into separate rooms. Kira turned to look at Luke as they were ushered into the rooms. Her eyes showed panic and Luke threw her a knowing half-smile. She guessed that he hadn't expected this either.

Kira was instructed to sit down by one of the female wardens. She figured that this meant she was the one with highest ranking. Kira's mind was trailing off with her thoughts and the female warden noticed.

'Look Kira, can I call you Kira?'

Kira nodded.

'Kira, my name is Anneliese. I am not the enemy as you could have guessed there is a major issue going on with the Wrathlings.'

Kira felt a sudden boost in her ability to speak and bit back, 'Not sure you can call it an issue.'

'No, I agree. It was a wrong choice of phrase. But still there is also the problem that you shouldn't know about any of this. Non-born's aren't supposed to know about the Kingdoms or Wardens or indeed any of it.'

'So, what are you going to do to me?'

'There's not much we can do. Luke has broken many rules bringing you into all of this and not to mention the recklessness he has exhibited by entering the King of Wrath's domain without prior authorisation from the council and the King himself.'

Kira grew concerned and shrunk back in the chair, 'Is he going to be alright?'

Anneliese shrugged, 'The council have yet to decide what to do about all of this. As you can imagine they are quite busy with dealing with the Wrathlings and the loss of the main stronghold. But Luke does have it on his side that he is one of the strongest fighters the Wardens have. So, he may get a pardon from being exiled.'

'Oh.' Kira's face filled with sadness. She didn't want Luke to be exiled. *After all, where would they exile him too? Especially when all he has done is kept her alive. Not sure that requires punishment.*

Anneliese assessed Kira with her eyes and tutted aloud.

'He's got you hasn't he.'

Kira was taken aback, 'Pardon?'

'Luke, he's got you wrapped around his finger. The whole caring and compassionate angle. He's managed to get you to have feelings for him.'

'What? No. He's Leons brother.'

'So, you are telling me that you don't have feelings for him? Could have fooled me.'

Anneliese knelt down next to Kira. 'Look Kira, you seem like a nice person, and I don't want you to be fooled by him. He isn't who you think he is. In fact, he even had a nickname back at the academy, giocare ragazzo. Play-boy'

'He doesn't act like a play-boy to me.'

'That's because he's playing you. Trust me. Luke is no good. Steer clear of him. Would you like a drink?'

Kira accepted the offer of a drink and Anneliese left her alone in the room. It was the first time that Kira had looked around the room properly. It was clear that it was a makeshift interrogation room as it looked like it was normally used as an office for paperwork or meetings. It had various paintings hung on either side of the room and a shelf which housed an open book. Kira got up and investigated.

The book was open and showed elaborately drawn family trees dating back centuries for the main family lines. She scoured through its pages and came across Luke and Leon's family tree, *The Wards*. Then she flicked further into the book and came across an unusual tree that ended back in the Elizabethan era. There was a question mark underneath one of the names where it would have been the date of death. Kira traced the tree with her fingers and read the title, 'The Guardians of Hell.'

Chapter Eleven

There was a stench of death in the air. It clung to everything, seeping into clothes and fabric. Contaminating all it touched. The last guardian tower had been breached. It was only a matter of time until she was found. She was sweating profusely. The news had travelled about the other towers being attacked but she thought she was safe. She was sure she was safe.

They had promised that it was a temporary measure. One needed to right the wrong-doings and that all would be well. But instead, it had turned into the massacre of her people. For what was just a misunderstanding. It was never supposed to get this far. But they had become blood thirsty, hungry for vengeance for fallen kin that was never her people's fault. But they needed someone to blame.

The first strike happened during the moon festival, what should have been a celebration of life was full of blood-shed and tears. Her people started to fight back. But they were no match against the sheer number of enemies. They were once trusted with all of the guardians' secrets; they knew all of her peoples powers and weapons and they were sure to attack those first. They laid traps and invented new weapons that would absorb their powers and leave them defenceless. They were no match.

She could hear boots running up and down the corridors. She clutched at her gown. Then there was silence. She let out a sigh but had to quickly stifle herself, covering her mouth as the door handle began to shake.

They were coming for her. She was powerless to stop them. In a mere few months, she had gone from being the most feared and powerful guardian to the fearful creature who cowered behind her bed posts.

She knew what the fates had in store for her and as much as she was surrounded by death she was not ready to welcome it. Smoke trickled in through the gaps in the door, The handle gave way and the interior doorknob fell to the floor. The door pushed open and the figure emerged from the bellowing smoke.

Her chest tightened and a lump formed in her throat. She wanted to scream but nothing would come out. The figure edged closer to her and a pain formed in her chest. Her pulse racing, she tried to back away from the figure, but it grabbed her in one swift movement. She fought against it, using her hands to hit and push to no avail.

Her head became dizzy but she could have sworn that she heard the sound of shattering glass and then nothing.

'Kira'

A sound reached out from the darkness. Kira stirred. Her eyes blurry, she focussed on the person in front of her. Anneliese was staring intensely at Kira.

'Kira what did you do? You're bleeding!'

Kira went to speak but then stopped, touched her head with her left hand, it came back covered in blood. 'I, I don't know what happened.'

Anneliese looked around to assess the situation. A painting that was hung up above the bookshelf had fallen off and now lay next to Kira, one of its corners had traces of blood on it. Anneliese picked it up and showed Kira,

'I think I know. You shouldn't be touching things that don't belong to your kind.'

'What on earth? Where did that come from??'

Kira glanced over the painting. She didn't remember seeing that in the room before.

Anneliese shrugged, 'It's always been here. It's an important painting of our history.'

Anneliese dabbed a tissue on Kira's forehead, 'The bleeding seems to be slowing down. Here.'

She shoved the tissue into Kira's hand for her to take over. Straightened herself up and went about putting the painting back.

Kira tilted her head and asked Anneliese about the painting. It depicted buildings ablaze and warriors with various weaponry. Then there was a woman in shackles, but she was dressed in a luxurious gown, with a high collar. Based on the clothing the painting looked to be from the Elizabethan era. Although it was definitely not taught during GCSE History.

Kira was caught up in her mind and only briefly caught what Anneliese was saying about the painting. She made out words like *triumphant victory* and *the last guardian.* The second one caught Kira's attention and she zoned in entirely on Anneliese.

'The last guardian?' Kira quizzed.

'Yes. This is the painting showing the fall of the guardians. Despite the name they were not guardians. They were evil beings who misled Wardens, made malicious pacts with demons and caused the death of our leader.'

Anneliese tossed her hair back and folded her arms against her chest. Her eyes narrowing. 'Enough of that anyway, best not to dwell on the past. We won and that's all that matters.'

Kira was transfixed by the painting and Anneliese's words reverberated through her. *We won. Evil beings. Malicious.*

Kira felt her teeth cling together and her body tense. The words kept circling in her mind. Her nostrils filled with the smell of death and smoke. She felt the terror as she continued to look at the painting. Kira's eyes turned cold. Her fists clenched. *Malicious.* Her breath quickened. *Evil beings.*

Anneliese turned and went to grab the drink that she had brought Kira just as the painting started to burn. It went up quickly and then the cremated artwork fell the floor, its ashes spreading upwards like a cloud.

Kira shifted and stood up, brushing the ash off of her face and clothes. Her body felt a wash of relief and her hands relaxed. Anneliese was in shock. Other guards came rushing in but there was nothing for them to do on arrival. The painting had gone and so had the flames.

Chapter Twelve

Anneliese was pacing the corridor, outside of the room. Adrastus had his arms folded. His face scornful.

'So, you are telling me. That somehow. Whilst under your care and supervision. That this. This human made a painting combust?'

Anneliese stopped pacing, 'Adrastus, I don't know what more I can tell you. She seemed to completely zone out and then clenched her fists, which glowed might I add. And then as if by magic, the painting went up in flames. That's literally all there is to it.'

He walked off without so much as a word and when he returned, he had brought six more guardians with him.

'Anneliese I can confirm your version of the event is true. We checked the camera in the room. Which means she is a hazard to us all and must be detained for further investigation.'

The group of six wardens rushed into the room and restrained Kira. They carted her off to the detention cells without informing her of a single thing. Kira let out a guttural scream.

Luke, who remained in the other interrogation room heard the scream as it bounced down the corridor. He instantly knew that it belonged to Kira. He grabbed one of the chairs and launched it at the door. There were no windows in the room, so he had to hope that there was someone stupid enough to risk coming into the room whilst he was enraged.

Luke was a well-known skilled fighter and there wasn't a soul at the academy that would have taken him on back then. Less so now that he'd had years to polish his skill set.

The door unlocked and opened. Apparently, there was someone daft enough to unlock the door whilst Luke was in his current state. Caiden entered the room. His face emblazoned with a smug smile; his blonde curly hair pruned to perfection. Caiden could fight, Luke would give him that, but Caiden never fought fair, and he certainly hadn't fought against Luke. Caiden locked the door behind him and approached Luke, puffing his chest out with his fists ready to swing.

Luke and Caiden exchanged several blows, most of Caiden's were completely off target but Luke managed to land several of his which knocked Caiden off balance, and he fell back into the wall. Caiden pressed an alarm which was in his pocket and within seconds Luke was surrounded by Wardens all of which were ready to strike. Adrastus entered.

'It really didn't need to come to this Luke. I was working with the council on getting you a full pardon for the crimes you have committed and by bringing the non-born into this. You truly have disappointed me. I think of you like a son and this. This is what you do to your family?'

Luke refused to calm down. His whole body fuelled by rage.

'My family are all dead. Or had you just forgotten that? The Wrathlings are on the loose and have literally just slain an entire stronghold and you are worried about me? You are disappointed in me? You should be disappointed in yourself. You are holding me up in here, for what? A display of power? Or to avoid your responsibility to the world to control the demons?'

Adrastus scorned, 'Do not cross me, Luke. I have been lenient thus far.'

Luke squared up to Adrastus, 'Lenient. How lenient have you been with Kira? Or did I just imagine her screams?'

The other Wardens edged near, but Adrastus signalled for them to stand down.

Adrastus stepped back and straightened his jacket before masking his emotions with a feigned attempt at an authoritative voice, 'She is a threat and a liability. She is to remain in our custody until the council determines her fate.'

Luke scoffed, 'A liability.' He pushed Adrastus and headed for the door. His one thought was on making sure Kira was okay. He didn't like the way Adrastus was referring to her. He didn't want anyone to ever speak ill of her. *Her.*

He shoved the other Wardens and bolted out of the door. The other Wardens were about to pursuit when Adrastus called them back. 'He's going nowhere.'

Luke was too occupied with thoughts of her that he hadn't noticed that he wasn't being followed. He had made it to the end of the corridor with a set of double doors. He pushed the door and felt a shock of lightning run through him. His hair standing on end and searing pain coursing through his veins.

He fell to the floor. Paralysed with pain he was still conscious enough to remember seeing Adrastus command two Wardens to drag his body to a cell.

Kira had spent the last two hours kicking the metal railings of the cell. It hadn't been fruitful in any shape or form, but it gave her something to do, and the sound of the clanging and rattling was annoying the guard on shift. Which she figured was fruitful, at least for entertainment purposes. The guard walked off with a huff. Kira guessed that it was change over time and it gave her a new victim to annoy. She rolled her eyes. Anneliese again.

Anneliese sauntered up to the cell door and grinned. 'Hi Kira.'

Kira pushed her tongue up against her teeth, 'Don't hi Kira me -okay? We're not friends and it is because of people like you that I am in this cell. I didn't want anything to do with this whole Hell fiasco but here I am.'

Anneliese avoided rising to it, which was saying a lot because she was very strong willed and wasn't known for having a good temperament, 'Will you just stop for a minute.'

Kira turned her back to the cell railings, '…and give you the pleasure of peace and quiet? Look, I am usually a polite, timid person but a lot has happened, I'm exhausted and royally peeved. So just go away.'

'Look, Luke is in cell E. Do with that what you will but here..' she unlocked the door and handed Kira the key to cell E.

'Why are you helping me?' quizzed Kira, who knew better than to trust strangers. Anneliese pulled a stool closer to the cell and sat on it cross-legged, twirling her hair with her fingers.

'I'm not. I do things that suit me and serve me a purpose. This does both. I don't like you because you are hogging all of the attention and I don't like Luke. So, you can let him out and he'll be on the run for the rest of his life or you can let him rot in a cell, either suits me just fine.' She placed both of her hands on her knee.

'Just know that if you want to be stupid enough to believe everything, he tells you and this persona that he cares so much about family.'

Kira froze. A pit formed in her stomach. She hated how Anneliese was talking about Luke, but she continued to listen.

'Tell me Kira, why is it you knew nothing about Luke before he saved you? Why has Luke never told you that Leon was supposed to inherit everything if his parents ever died. And how convenient is it that Leon's gone and so are both of Luke's parents? Who is the bad guy really? Me? For telling you the truth? Or Luke for keeping secrets? Just some food for thought for you.'

Kira stood for a few seconds with the key in her hand. She could let Luke out, after-all he did save her from numerous Wrathling attacks, but she had also saved his ass plenty too. Still, she had a gut feeling that she somehow owed him, but Anneliese's words had struck a chord and she found herself questioning Luke's intentions.

She was right, she had never even heard of Luke before the first attack, but Leon had also not told her about who he truly was either. It also seemed a little convenient that Luke would technically now inherit everything but what was left to inherit? His house was up in flames.

Kira clawed at her head. *Why was nothing ever easy?*

Anneliese started tapping her foot impatiently. 'Look, are you going or not? There's a five-minute window where you can leave so decide and go.'

Kira nodded. She wasn't sure what the window was caused by but she wasn't sure she would get this chance again, so she headed out. She followed very helpful signage and headed towards cell E. Her head was uncertain about a lot of things, but she knew that if Luke was dealt the choice, he would have come for her.

Chapter Thirteen

Kira had located the entrance to the block of cells where Luke was being kept. The door was cool against her hands, she hesitated. She wasn't sure what she was feeling but she sensed that something felt *off*.

Now would have been a good time to own a watch. How long has it been since I left my cell? Kira pondered and pushed open the entry door. Luke was curled up in a ball in the far corner of his cell. She had never seen him like this, so distraught and vulnerable. She reached out to him and called for his attention. She unlocked his cell, and he ran to her. His whole demeanour changed when he saw her and embraced her in a hug.

'Are you okay?' she asked him.

'I am now that I know you are okay.'

He smiled although it appeared to pain him to do so. He winced when he let her go from the embrace.

Kira spoke hurriedly, 'We have to go.'

Luke led the way as he claimed to be familiar with the layout of the safehouse. Although they did end up with a few dead ends along the way but not before long, fresh air was brushing against their faces and the breeze swept through Kira's hair which was now matted with sweat, ash and a whole host of things she didn't want to think about.

A lone Warden who was returning to the safehouse clocked the duo but backed away with fear, 'I don't want any trouble,' muttered the Warden as he raised his hands up and stepped aside.

Luke eyed the Warden up and down, his face intimidating.

'Do you have a vehicle?'

The lone Warden nodded and swallowed hard. His body trembling. He fished the keys out of his top pocket and threw them to the floor. Kicking them over to Luke. Luke thanked him for his cooperation and headed to the parking facility. They located the car and started its engine. In the distance, blurry figures were heading straight towards them. *I guess our window is up.*

'Floor it,' she commanded Luke and the car, a turquoise BMW squealed and sped off, leaving a trail of dust.

Luke turned to Kira, 'We need to ditch the car.'

Kira protested, 'But we need a vehicle.'

He sighed and nodded. But she knew that he was also right. Luke spotted a nearby ravine and parked up facing it. He put the car in neutral and instructed Kira to help him push it into the ravine. The car rolled and fell into the gorge. The headlights shining away in the darkness.

Luke guided Kira through a clearing and found a well rooted and overgrown tree to lay under. The night was clear and the air was warm. Kira settled down to sleep and Luke began the first watch. He had nothing but admiration for Kira. She was a strong, fierce woman with a compassionate soul. She had literally been to Hell and back, faced many a demon but still managed to ask him if he was the one that was okay.

His pupils dilated as he watched her fall asleep. Her breathing slowing as she drifted off further and further into a deep slumber. They were now pariahs and whilst he couldn't guarantee her overall safety, he could ensure that at least for tonight, she had a safe sleep. For tomorrow, they would need to journey back his home to get supplies and only Hell knows what is in store for them when they get there.

Kira awoke to deafening screams. She clutched at her ears and looked around. Her surroundings were different, and Luke was nowhere to be seen. She called out for him but there was no answer. Bits of ash fell from the sky like tiny raindrops, clutching to her skin.

She brushed them off and continued to look around. The sky was murky with a strange orange tint, there was no presence of a sun or a moon yet visibility was mostly clear, except for the light dusting of ash. The scream came again and she clutched back at her ears, and then it stopped. Instead of a scream this time it was a desperate plea, a shout for help. The voice was familiar, a little huskier but a voice she knew all too well. Kira gasped and ran in the direction of the sound.

There, suspended from the ceiling in an iron cage was a man. He was bloody and bruised, his clothes were ripped and torn. A thick layer of ash covered his hair and skin, but he was still identifiable. *Leon.*

Kira instinctively ran to him and looked for a way to bring the cage down to the ground. She tried to clutch at the lever which would return him to her, but she couldn't get it to move. Two heavily disfigured Wrathlings appeared. Both looked like they had seen more than a fair share of battles and had been severely wounded from them. Their claws still razor sharp and their teeth just the same. Their glowing red eyes fixated on the lever Kira was stood next to.

Kira panicked but was unable to move. Fixed in place she waited for her end to come as the Wrathlings came towards her.

The Wrathlings went straight for the lever and didn't even notice Kira stood next to it. *That's strange,* Kira thought to herself as she watched them. The first Wrathling let the cage down as the second went to retrieve large spears. He handed a spear to his comrade and they both approached Leon's cage.

Despite Kira's protests, they each took it in turns to prod Leon with the spears, to which he let out an excruciating howl each time the spear head connected with his body. Kira's protests grew louder and louder, but they didn't bat an eyelid in her direction. Her fists started to clench and emit a purple light.

Kira could feel herself being pulled backwards. Her feet dragging along the floor as she was pulled further and further away from Leon. She dug her heels in, but it was no use.

Darkness consumed her. She fought back and used all of her energy to hit and claw at her attacker.

'Ow. Kira. Stop!' cried out her attacker and she stopped. She blinked hard a few times and focussed herself. She was staring at a very pained Luke.

'You were crying out in your sleep and then, well your hand started to change colour and I knew I had to wake you.'

'I. I was asleep?' Kira's eyes flooded with sadness as the realisation that it was just a dream sunk in.

Kira relayed all of the details to Luke. Who offered her comfort and reassurance that Leon was now at peace. That it was all just a terrifying nightmare. Kira rested her head on his lap and the pair lay in silence waiting for the sun to rise.

Kira stretched and wiped the sleep from her eyes. It had been exhausting and although she was scared to drift off again, she must have been so sleep deprived that she had just dozed off. She sat up after realising she had fallen asleep on Luke, but it appeared that he had also fallen asleep as he was still snoring. She politely elbow jabbed him to wake him up but instead he leapt up and let out a howl.

'I didn't elbow you that hard,' stated Kira who was scowling at him.

Luke rubbed at his ribs and winced. Kira's face changed from playful scowling to a look of concern. She stood up and placed her hand on his left ribs. He withdrew from her touch. Kira spoke softly, 'Let me see.'

Luke took a deep breath and removed his shirt. His eyes scrunched as he lifted it over his head. His body was purple and blue, with heavy swelling. Small lightning shaped veins spread from his left side all the way along his spine. Kira gently traced them with her fingers. Luke turned and grabbed her hands.

She tilted her head and looked him in the eyes, 'What did *they* do to you?'

His eyes were filled with sadness, 'Kira it's fine, it's done now.'

Kira felt overwhelmed. She was still trying to work out her feelings for Luke as well as dealing with the news of Hell and the loss of Leon. But seeing him like this, so vulnerable, so open. A tear fell from her eye, she looked down to try to cover it, but Luke tilted her chin up with his finger, his right hand still holding her left hand firmly. He leaned in and kissed the tear that sat on her cheek. Kira's heart started to race. *Why does being with Luke feel oh so right?*

He used the hold on her chin to direct her lips to his. Kissing her with raw passion, she could sense that he had been longing for her as much as she had for him. Her stomach doing somersaults. Luke stepped back timidly and ran his hands through his hair, blushing at how forward he was. *But she had kissed him back…*

Kira was breathless following their passionate make-out. Each of them staring at the other, neither one quite sure how to approach what had just happened between them. A twig broke in the distance and caused Luke to ready himself for action. Kira tossed him his shirt and he threw it on. His gaze never leaving the direction of the sound.

Chapter Fourteen

There was another snapped twig followed by the crunching sound of leaves. This time the sounds came from the opposite direction. Kira turned. There were more crunching sounds, each time they came from a new direction. The sun was only just rising, and the trees provided vast coverage, the shadows keeping the area dark and shaded.

Hair started to stand up on the back of Kira's neck, travelling down her arms. She felt uneasy. Glancing over to Luke, she knew that he felt it too. They were being watched. Unsure if they were being watched by Wrathlings,

Wardens or something else entirely, they stood their ground, waiting.

Kira and Luke shifted so that they were back-to-back, weapon-less but ready. They were outnumbered, with at least twelve Wrathlings now circling them. These creatures were unlike any they had ever encountered before. They were small, about the size of a child, but their skin was a blue and green hue. As with all Wrathlings, their eyes glowed a fierce red.

The Wrathlings started to move in closer, edging nearer and nearer, their sharp claws clicking against the ground. Kira and Luke knew that they had to be careful. The Wrathlings were fast and agile, and their teeth and claws could do serious damage.

Kira took a deep breath, trying to steady her nerves. She had faced many dangers on her travels, but this felt different. There was something more primal and menacing about these creatures that made her skin crawl. *How did the Wrathlings know where they were? Luke had mentioned previously that they – for lack of a better phrase- had few brain cells.*

Suddenly, one of the Wrathlings lunged forward, its claws outstretched. Luke managed to dodge out of the way, but another one came at him from behind. Kira stepped forward, swinging a large branch, knocking another of the Wrathlings over. The Wrathling dropped an ornate dagger as it tumbled to the ground. Kira grabbed it and sliced through the Wrathling's arm, causing it to screech in pain.

The other Wrathlings started to attack, their claws and teeth gnashing at Kira and Luke. It was a fierce battle, with both sides trading blows. Kira could feel her muscles burning as she fought, but she refused to give up. Armed with the ornate dagger she powered through.

Finally, after what felt like hours, the last of the Wrathlings lay still on the ground. Kira and Luke were battered and bruised, but they had emerged victorious in spite of the odds they were dealt.

They stood there for a moment, panting and catching their breath, assessing the aftermath. Kira looked around at the bodies of the Wrathlings, feeling a mix of relief and revulsion. Luke put a hand on her shoulder, his voice low and reassuring. 'We did it,' he said. 'We survived.'

Kira nodded, her heart still pounding. She knew that they had many more dangers ahead, but for now, she was grateful to be alive. She turned to Luke with a small but genuine smile. 'Let's keep moving,' she said. 'We have a long way to go.'

Luke and Kira searched for a mode of transportation to return to the stronghold, determined to find the King of Wrath. It was the only way to redeem themselves with Adrastus and other wardens. They knew it was a risky move, but with nothing to lose, they were willing to take the chance.

Luke and Kira arrived at a large fenced field, hoping to find a means of transportation back to the stronghold. They discovered a large shed that appeared to be run-down and abandoned. The shed's roof was in desperate need of repair, and the lock on the front door was old and rusted.

Despite their initial hesitation to enter, Luke and Kira decided to push the rusted lock open. The door creaked loudly as it gave way, and they stepped inside. Their eyes took a moment to adjust to the dimly lit interior of the shed, but once they did, they saw that it was filled with various items.

Luke rummaged around, looking for anything that could be useful. He found empty paint cans, old horseshoes, cobwebs, and dust sheets. He sifted through various old magazines that were in a state of deterioration due to weathering and old age. After some time, he stumbled upon an old shotgun that seemed to be in working condition.

Meanwhile, Kira noticed something of interest towards the left side of the shed. She walked over and removed an old blue tarp sheet that had been covering a bulky object. To her surprise, the object was an old quad bike, and the keys dangled from the ignition.

Feeling hopeful, Kira turned the quad bike's key, and to her relief, it started. She called out to Luke, who rushed over to her side. Together, they realised that the old quad bike was their ticket out of the shed and back to the stronghold. They quickly hopped onto the bike and rode away in search of the King of Wrath.

After a tremendous journey that spanned several hours, Kira and Luke had finally arrived at the entrance of the stronghold. The building, which once stood tall and majestic, now lay in ruins, a casualty of the horrific war that had ravaged through the land.

Looking at the destruction wrought upon his home, Luke could feel anger and sadness churn within him. The Wrathlings and their King had a lot to answer for, and the devastation they caused demanded justice.

In the midst of his pain, Kira could sense how deeply Luke felt about his ruined home and the loss of his family. Her heart went out to him for all the loss and suffering he had been through at the hands of the enemy.

Kira and Luke made their way towards one of the outbuildings, grateful to find that it had somehow remained untouched by the battle with the Wrathlings. Despite their stroke of luck, they approached with caution, aware of the dangers that may be lurking. Bracing themselves, they gingerly stepped inside, scanning the area for any signs of danger.

Their eyes soon fell upon the supplies and weaponry scattered throughout the room, and their hearts leapt with relief. Picking through the gear, they gathered everything they deemed necessary for the journey ahead, hesitant to leave any potential advantage behind. They knew that they were venturing into treacherous territory, and they needed to be as prepared as possible to face whatever lay ahead.

Kira thought back to their previous encounter in the kingdom of Wrath, Kira and Luke had faced a situation that had left them vulnerable. It had been a close call, and they had only emerged victorious by the skin of their teeth. As they set out on their journey once more, they were filled with a sense of unease, knowing that they could not afford to make any mistakes if they hoped to survive the dangers that lay ahead.

Kira's eyes widened in surprise as Luke showed her a small purple vial, its iridescent glass sparkling.

Luke proudly announced, 'This grants us the power of invisibility'.

'Where did you find that?' she asked, amazed.

'I found it buried amongst some old crates,' replied Luke with a grin, 'I wasn't expecting to find anything quite like this, but this changes everything.'

Kira nodded, her mind already racing with plans for how they could use the vial to their advantage.

'This is a game-changer,' she said. 'We can use it to sneak through undetected.'

Luke half-smiled in agreement.

'But we need to be careful,' he warned. 'The vial won't last forever, and if we're caught, we'll be in serious trouble.'

Kira bowed her head, understandingly, 'We'll use it wisely,' she said resolutely. 'And make every moment count.'

With renewed determination, Kira and Luke set off, their minds focused on the formidable task at hand. They knew that the journey ahead would be fraught with danger, but with the vial of invisibility on their side, they felt more confident than ever before.

Chapter Fifteen

At the start of their journey, the duo had an easy time navigating the courtyard and remaining undetected as they made their way towards the stronghold's ground zero. However, Kira's anxiety persisted despite their apparent success, and every time they passed a Wrathling, her heart would race with fear. It seemed that the Wardens had already given up and abandoned the ruined building, much to the delight of the ever-hungry Wrathlings.

Walking past them was a haunting experience, as their fiery eyes seemed to penetrate straight through Kira, leaving her feeling exposed and vulnerable. The overall atmosphere of the encounter was both eerie and unsettling.

They arrived at ground zero to find an empty room with only faint scorch marks remaining, the earlier destruction had been swept away. As they attempted to move towards the door to Wrath's kingdom, they encountered a large Wrathling blocking their path. The Wrathling's massive size and red, furious eyes caused Kira to feel unnerved and shiver with fear. There was something about the way the eyes were watching her that made her feel uneasy.

The Wrathling let out a sound which erupted into a thunderous roar, slamming its massive, clawed hands against the walls. Kira stumbled backward, feeling the ground shake beneath her feet. She steadied herself as Luke quickly pulled out his shotgun realising that their time undetected had come to an end.

He fired a shot at the creature, but it seemed unaffected and only became angrier. The Wrathling charged at them, forcing Luke to toss aside his shotgun and draw his sword while Kira turned to see another Wrathling lurking in the shadows, grinning menacingly with more joining the ambush.

The duo fought fiercely against the Wrathlings, as each one took turns lashing, clawing, and lunging at the pair. Kira's inexperience with weaponry was no hindrance as she fought with the sword as if it came to her naturally. However, they were outmatched against the ever-increasing number of Wrathlings.

Luke found himself sandwiched between two of the creatures, tearing and clawing at him with ferocity, ripping his clothes and skin. He swayed under the weight of his injuries, struggling to keep fighting against the onslaught. Kira leapt forward, slashing at the Wrathlings with her sword, fighting to defend herself whilst trying to reach Luke.

But as they fought, it became apparent that they would soon be overrun and overwhelmed. The reinforcements of Wrathlings were too many for just two people. They had walked straight into a ruthless and calculated ambush and needed to escape before it was too late. Kira looked around for a way to escape but saw no opportunity, they were doomed.

Luke was losing his battle and Kira had no way to get to him as she too faced the army of Wrathlings. Her heart was beating furiously, panting as she fought for her life.

Suddenly, without warning, Kira slammed her hand onto the ground, causing the floor to crack open and fiery flames from the depths of hell to erupt from the earth's surface. The Wrathlings were consumed, leaving only scorch marks as remnants of their existence. Kira ran over to Luke and cradled him in her arms as he bled from his injuries. Luke gradually regained consciousness and was stunned by the sight before him.

With the threat eliminated, Luke and Kira prepared to leave. The flames that had once raged and threatened to incinerate them not long before were now reduced to smouldering embers.

Kira patched Luke up with makeshift bandages from torn cloth, with the reassurance that he would heal quickly due to not being completely human. They made their way to the door and descended down to Wraths kingdom. The earlier trip had been unsuccessful as they were informed that Wrath was not there. However, if Wrath was unavailable then they would speak directly to his second in command and demand an audience with the King. This time they would not leave until they had come face to face with the King himself.

Kira took a deep breath; the staircase still haunted her and made her queasy at the thought of walking all over the bones of another human. Well, she supposed that they were made entirely of human remains, but Hell had a funny way of surprising her.

The kingdom of Wrath, once filled with life and prosperity, now lay in ruins. Barren and desolate, it looked nothing like the place Kira remembered from her previous visit. Everywhere they looked, signs of abandonment and decay met their eyes. Not a soul could be seen as they ventured further into the Kingdom, and the only sound was the howling of the wind as it whipped through the empty streets and fields.

Kira's heart sank as she realised that their journey had been for nothing once again. She had fought hard to seek out the truth behind the Wrathlings' attacks, to bring justice for Leon, Luke, and all the others who had suffered at their hands. She had risked everything, only to find an empty, lifeless wasteland.

Tears welled up in Kira's eyes as she struggled to process the mixed emotions that were overwhelming her. Her fury turned to sadness as she wondered if she would ever find the answers she so desperately sought. Luke, too, was consumed with anger, and he lashed out at a nearby tree with his fists, his knuckles splitting and blood starting to trickle down his arms.

In defeat, Kira turned and began to head back up the staircase, feeling as if all their efforts had been in vain. But as she and Luke made their way back, they heard a sound that made them freeze in their tracks.

The sound slowly grew louder and louder until it filled the barren surroundings. Kira's heart started to race as she recognized the familiar voice. She couldn't believe it - was it really him? Her mind couldn't comprehend, but her heart knew all too well. The voice belonged to none other than *Leon*.

Luke's eyes widened as he heard the same voice. His brother was alive!
The anger and sadness that had taken over him just moments ago dissipated, replaced by a surge of hope and elation. He had lost so much and so many people, if Leon was still *alive*…a sense of relief washed over him.

As Leon's voice grew louder, it filled the air with its distinctive timbre, resounding off the walls of the desolate kingdom. Kira couldn't contain her tears as she realised that they had not journeyed in vain after all. They may not have gotten the answers they were searching for but for a small moment there was hope. They had heard his voice, Leon was alive, and he was *here*, in Wraths Kingdom.

Chapter Sixteen

Their hope renewed, they followed the sound, their hearts racing with anticipation. Down the staircase of bones they went, their minds filled with the possibilities of what they might find. They were determined to find Leon, no matter what.

As they descended further and further into the depths of Wrath's Kingdom, their flashlight illuminating the way, they came across a cavern that was hidden by broken branches and dead trees. Following Leon's voice, they made their way towards the cavern, ready to face whatever they might find inside.

What they saw was chilling. An empty cage, suspended from the top of the cavern, rusted iron bars and chains. Kira and Luke looked at each other, their minds filled with thoughts of Kira's nightmare, the exact same room she had described in vivid detail.

How was this even possible? Could Kira's dream have been a premonition of things to come? They couldn't be sure, but something told them that this was more than a coincidence.

They searched the cavern, looking for any clues that might help them find Leon. Their hearts pounding with fear, but their minds set on their mission. They searched high and low, looking for any sign that would lead them to him. But the darkness had swallowed him whole, and there was no trace of him to be found.

But there was no evidence that he had even been there at all, except for what Kira saw in her dream. There was no blood, no pieces of his clothing. Nothing. They were about to turn around and head back out when Kira spotted something in the shadows. They both jumped to action ready to fight whatever came their way but were surprised to find that the shadows didn't move. They were still.

As Luke made his way closer to the shadows, the beam of the flashlight continuing to illuminate the way, Kira gasped. The shadows were as expected, Wrathlings, but they were already dead. It appeared that they had been dead for a while, as flies had already formed on the two corpses. They were heavily disfigured, but Kira had a gut instinct that these were the two Wrathlings from her dream.

As they turned to leave, breathing a sigh of relief that they had not come face to face with the living Wrathlings, they were greeted by a figure in black armour, standing between them and the exit. This was the Knight of Wrath, the sworn protector of the realm, and he was not happy to see them. The Knight was tall and well built, his armour emblazoned with engraved serpents and onyx stones. His eyes, like the Wrathlings, were red and he paraded around almost human-like. His face scarred from many battles.

Kira and Luke stood frozen in fear, unsure of what to do next. The Knight of Wrath was a formidable opponent, and Luke had heard stories of his incredible strength and battle prowess. But they were not ones to give up without a fight, and so they prepared for battle.

Luke stepped forward, taking the lead, his fists clenched tightly by his side. The Knight of Wrath drew his sword, his eyes fixed on Luke. The two began to circle each other, sizing each other up, waiting for the other to make the first move.

The Knight of Wrath attacked first, his sword slicing through the air with deadly precision. Luke dodged the blow, his agility and quick reflexes serving him well. He launched his own attack, his fists connecting with the Knight's armour with a resounding thud.

The battle raged on, Kira provided support and assistance wherever she could, occasionally landing blows of her own. The Knight caught her arm in one swift movement and threw her across the cavern, her back creating a resounding thud as it slammed into the wall. The Knight of Wrath was a formidable foe, but Luke was determined to come out on top, his mind focused on one thing: winning the battle and getting to safety.

As the battle intensified, Luke and the Knight of Wrath continued to trade blow for blow, neither of them backing down. Luke's strength and determination were impressive, but the Knight of Wrath was a tough adversary. It was a battle to the death, and there was no telling who would come out on top.

Finally, after what felt like an eternity, the Knight of Wrath was subdued. Luke had emerged victorious, his strength and determination paying off in the end. Kira and Luke breathed a sigh of relief, their hearts pounding with adrenaline and fear.

Together, they made their way to safety, their minds abuzz with thoughts of what had just happened. As they walked away from the darkness of the cavern and into the light, they couldn't help but feel a sense of triumph. They had fought against all odds and won, and they knew that they were stronger for it. The journey ahead might be long and treacherous, but they were ready for whatever lay ahead.

They needed to search for answers and there was only one person who could truly confirm if Leon was ever in the Kingdom of Wrath and that was the King himself. But they had yet to find his royal highness, so found themselves with limited options.

Luke sighed. He had not wanted to call upon him as he wasn't always reliable and due to not having any bias, there was also no guarantee that he wouldn't just hand them over to either side if he felt like it. Or if he could benefit from doing so. But, unlike Wrath, he knew exactly where to find him, and it was their last shot at getting to the King. It was only a matter of time before they were captured by either party, unable to run forever. Most importantly, he owed it to Kira and to Leon to get to the bottom of what had happened to his brother.

'Where do we go from here?' asked Kira in between deep breaths, still suffering from being flung across the cavern.

Luke hesitantly answered, 'to get Haruspex.'

Kira frowned, waiting for him to expand but Luke offered no further information. Instead, he dusted himself off, wiped his bloodied knuckles and continued to head out of the kingdom. Kira, not wanting to press any further, followed behind.

Chapter Seventeen

As Luke and Kira headed towards the entrance of ground zero to leave, they felt a small sense of relief that they had left the kingdom and got to the entrance with no further complications. Albeit with a slight sourness to it, having been unsuccessful in finding Wrath or Leon. However, their hope was short-lived as they arrived at a crumbling wall, which had obviously suffered from the earlier damage. Suddenly, a massive chunk of rock fell off the wall, hurtling down towards them.

Without hesitation, Luke sprang into action, grabbing Kira by the waist and pulling her out of harm's way. As he held her close in his arms, their eyes locked, and time seemed to stand still. In that moment, they realise just how much they meant to each other.

Feeling grateful to be alive and safe in each other's embrace, Kira rests her head against Luke's chest, listening to the sound of his heartbeat. As they come to their senses, they slowly pull away from each other and continue their journey, but the feeling of their bodies entwined remains etched in their minds.

Everything they had been through had brought them closer. Kira couldn't deny she had feelings for Luke, but she also had feelings for Leon and if Leon was still alive…she wasn't sure what that would mean for her and Luke. She had promised a lifetime to Leon, and she had no intentions of backing out of that promise. But her bond with Luke had grown even stronger in the face of adversity, and they both knew that they would do anything to protect each other.

Kira found herself mulling over her feelings for each brother. They were both so different. She found herself trying to list out their qualities, hoping that it would put her mind at ease, but it just made things harder.

Luke was secure, he made her feel safe but also allowed her to be independent, to make her own choices and respected her confidence and opinions. Leon made her feel wooed, he spoilt her, but he also removed responsibilities, he would make the decisions, so she didn't have to. She found herself considering that last point, unsure if it was actually a positive or a negative.

Whilst Kira was inside her head, Luke was busy moving debris from in front of the door. He shifted enough that it allowed him to pry the door partially open. He signalled for Kira to join him, and the pair pried the door open fully, enabling them to head up to the stronghold. Luke guided her down corridors and through room after room, determined to get to a particular part of the stronghold. He knew each twist and turn like the back of his hand which was helpful given that a lot of the rooms were destroyed beyond recognition. The stronghold now vacant, the Wrathlings had either moved on of their own accord or had heard about the defeat at ground zero.

Luke started to hammer at the wall. Occasionally, pressing his ear against the wall. 'I know it's here somewhere,' he muttered as he continued to tap his fist up and down the wall. Eventually his taps became hollow, and he pulled out a small pocketknife, scraping at the wallpaper. He found an edging and began to pull at it. Exposing a large wooden covering. He used the knife to dislodge the covering from the wall and it fell to the floor, revealing an old dumb waiter, the ropes still attached.

'Hop in,' announced Luke as he held out his hand for Kira to climb inside. It was only big enough for one person at a time and although Kira was unsure about being the first to go down, she also didn't want to hang around in-case any Wrathlings returned. Luke pulled at the rope, lowering her down and the dumb waiter travelled jerkily, it came to a halt and Kira slid up the wooden panel, stepping into a dusty, dimly lit room. An old oil lamp was burning in the far corner. Kira tugged at the rope and the dumb waiter went back up. She stood still, unmoving in-case whatever had lit the lamp came back. Luke appeared behind her.

Luke started to walk around the room, 'You could have taken a look around, you know.'

'I didn't know who else was in here.'

Luke looked from one side of the room to the other, it was clearly empty except for the pair of them, 'What do you mean?'

'The lamp?'

'Oh, that old thing. Yeah, that's always on. It's powered by Hell fire, so it never goes out. Quite nifty if you ask me.'

Kira looked at him dumbfounded. He said it in such a matter-of-fact way, like she should have known what it was. Luke looked over at her and realised his error, 'I forget that you don't know much about all of this. You just handle everything so well that it's like you've been here all along.'

Kira didn't know whether that was a compliment or Luke trying to cover up the fact that he completely forgot that she was new to all of this and may require a little more consideration. She sighed and ran her fingers along the side, studying the contents of the room. The room was well stocked with various objects, jars, an old bookcase, lots of scattered papers and a small loveseat style sofa, which would have once been jade green but had mostly discoloured over time. She wondered how old the room was.

Luke set about gathering a variety of objects and jars piling them onto the sofa each time, and then going back for more. Kira wandered over to the sofa and eyed up the objects, they all had labels but they were written in another language. 'What do we need these for?' she asked.

'To get Haruspex'

'What or who is this Haruspex?'

'An upper-level demon who doesn't take sides. He likes to keep his options open in order to get more business and trade.'

'His business is?'

'He's a seer. He can tell you things about the future. But it always comes with a cost or a deal. If you want something from him, he needs something from you. I didn't want to have to go to him, but we are running out of options and time. You just have to be careful in the questions you ask and the information you tell him. You don't want him giving the information away to your enemies.'

Luke knew that he needed to be precise in his actions; any deviation, any misstep could lead to disaster. He had studied the art of summoning for years, and he knew that this ritual could be the one that would help them find Wrath.

He carefully drew a perfect pentagram on the floor with a piece of charcoal, making sure that the lines were straight, and the angles were sharp. He wiped his brow, surveying the room and the collection of vials and jars that he had meticulously collected. Now, he was ready to begin.

He started to empty the contents of the jars and vials, one by one, into a circle around the outside of the pentagram. Each one contained something unique and potent, something that would enhance the power of the ritual.

He poured a thick, red liquid that smelt strongly of iron out of one jar onto the floor. One by one the contents were emptied. As he worked, he chanted incantations in a language that no one had spoken for centuries. He concentrated hard, careful to get the words just right. The candles that were placed around the room flickered as if they were alive, drawn towards the circle he had created.

Luke felt the room surge with power which grew with each passing minute. He was channelling energies from other planes of existence, weaving them into a potent web that would help him in summoning Haruspex.

When all the jars and vials had been emptied, he stood back and closed his eyes, focusing his willpower on the pentagram in front of him, keeping his intent clear. The air around him grew thick with tension as he concentrated, sweat forming on his forehead.

Suddenly, the centre of the pentagram erupted in a bright flash of purple light, and a dark figure appeared, wreathed in smoke and shadows. It was the upper-level demon Haruspex, summoned to them.

The demon laughed, a chill running down Luke's spine. He knew that he had to be careful, as he was unpredictable and dangerous.

Chapter Eighteen

Haruspex stepped straight out of the pentagram and smiled, 'You honestly didn't think that little parlour trick could contain me?'

Luke stepped back, his arm stretched out in front of Kira, shielding her.

Haruspex chuckled, 'Now, now little Warden. It wouldn't benefit my business if I went about killing potential customers now, would it?'

He kicked back on the sofa, stretching his legs across the entire length of the chair.

After taking a relaxed posture, Haruspex asked, 'Why have you summoned me today?'

His question made Luke and Kira even more uneasy, as they did not expect Haruspex to be so casual given that he was a high-powered demon. For someone with such a prolific history who was known by the Wardens to be so dangerous, he looked incredibly charming and down to earth. He was dressed smartly, in a navy-blue suit with a white shirt, however he left the collar unfastened which made his appearance more laid back, his blonde hair shaggy and somewhat unkempt. But what captured Kira was his bright violet eyes, the irises seeming to dance under the candlelight. If it wasn't for those, you could have sworn that he was just some rich kid, looking no older than twenty-one living off of a family trust fund.

Despite their apprehension, they knew they had to keep their composure and try to extract some vital information from him. So, they cautiously explained that they needed his help in tracking down the King of Wrath as the Wrathlings were wreaking havoc and had caused countless deaths. Haruspex listened intently to their request, and as he did so, an enigmatic smile played on his lips, suggesting that he was intrigued by their proposal.

'So, you have informed me what you want but what do I get in return for helping you with this task?'

Luke hesitated, he wasn't sure what the demon would want or what he could offer. Haruspex nodded and started to speak, 'Look, let's be honest here. I'm not daft and I know what's been going on. I knew you would be asking for my help way before you summoned me so let's cut to the chase. I will do what you ask of me if I can have five minutes alone with her'.

'What no way!' outraged Luke stepped in front of Kira, but she moved aside and accepted Haruspex's proposal.

He smiled, 'Unlike you. She has sense.'

Luke huffed and pursed his lips together, his teeth clenching. He didn't agree with Kira's decision, but he had to respect it. Haruspex offered his hand to Kira, she took it and the pair disappeared in a flash of light, leaving Luke stood in the room on his own. They had only been gone for five minutes but Luke was becoming increasingly nervous. He wanted to know why Haruspex wanted to speak to her without his presence.

The room began to shake, bottles falling over, and pieces of paper flew off the sides. The candles blew out as Haruspex and Kira returned; the only light that remained came from the eternal Hell fire flame. Luke rushed to check over Kira who was unharmed. Haruspex resumed sitting on the sofa, smiling.

'So, now that's done. I have written down the information you need to find his royal highness. But just so you are aware, things aren't quite what they seem.' He handed Luke a piece of paper with the location to Wrath written down in neat penmanship. Luke looked it over and frowned.

'What do you mean things aren't what they seem?' Luke asked, trying to sound firm.

Haruspex's playful smirk turned into a serious expression that caused Kira's heart to skip a beat. She couldn't help but feel uneasy around the powerful warlock who seemed to know more than he was letting on. Luke, on the other hand, was trying to maintain his composure and act strong. He knew that Haruspex could sense fear and that showing it would only give him an advantage.

Haruspex's face lightened and he chuckled, 'Oh, little Warden, you have no idea what's coming. This world is on the brink of chaos, and you and your kind will be caught in the middle of it all. People, like me, are not the only ones who possess hidden powers. There are forces out there that are beyond your comprehension. One's that even I wouldn't dare face against.'

Kira looked at Luke, hoping for an explanation, but he seemed just as confused as her. Haruspex's cryptic words only added to her ever-growing list of stress and anxiety.

'Then, what do we do?' Luke asked, hoping that Haruspex would have a solution.
'You can't stop what's coming, but you can prepare for it,' Haruspex emphasized. 'You need to be ready for the battle that is coming. It won't be won easily, and many will die, but it is essential to keep fighting.'

Luke and Kira were still trying to wrap their heads around what Haruspex was saying when he stood up from the sofa and walked towards them. They instinctively took a step back, but Haruspex just smiled.

'Relax, little ones. Like I have already said, I'm not here to harm you, not yet anyway," Haruspex chuckled. 'I just wanted to give you a little warning. The future is uncertain, but one thing is for sure: you will play a significant role in the events to come.'

With that, Haruspex walked back towards the pentagram and disappeared in blaze of flames, leaving Kira and Luke alone with their thoughts. They both knew in their hearts that the battle Haruspex spoke of was not far away, and they needed to prepare for the worst. The fate of their world depended on it. Luke turned to face Kira as he asked about what Haruspex had wanted her for.

Kira smiled, 'he wanted to know who my parents were'.

'That's all?'

'Yep.'

Luke rubbed his brow, it seemed a strange request for a high-powered demon to make but then again from the stories he had heard about Haruspex, it shouldn't have surprised him as he was known to make unusual requests.

Chapter Nineteen

Kira didn't like lying to Luke, but it was for the best. Haruspex had warned her that someone close to her couldn't be trusted and it wasn't worth the risk. It was true that he had asked her about her parent's, but the truth was that she didn't know who her parents were, she was put up for adoption shortly after she was born and after being adopted the adoption centre had a fire, so all her records were lost.

When she became old enough to ask her adoptive parents about her history and where she came from. She had already lost her adoptive Mum and her adoptive Dad became an alcoholic as he couldn't cope with the loss.

So, the questions that she had wanted to ask were never spoken and never answered.

Haruspex had given her an antique locket, it was nothing special, merely plain white gold on a white gold chain with an inscription which had faded over time. He told her to hold onto it and that when the time is right, she was to open it. She had asked how she would know when the time was right, but he simply replied to listen to her instincts and that she would *just* know.

Haruspex acted like he had an vested interest in her, and she couldn't quite work out why. How someone she had never met, let alone a renowned demon, would show a special interest in her. How he wanted to know who her parents were.

She ran her fingers over the locket which was hidden away in her pocket. Luke was replenishing their supplies and ransacking boxes to find other things that may be useful. He found an old GPS which had enough battery to allow him to punch in the location given by Haruspex. As soon as he had entered the location in, the piece of paper combusted in his hand, Luke dropping it as the flames licked his fingers.

Luke tried to lighten the tension in the air, there was a lot riding on them getting to

Wrath and holding him accountable, 'I guess he's one for parlour tricks'.

Kira half laughed, a small part of her felt a little relief, before the sinking feeling kicked back in. Lying to Luke was eating away at her but telling Luke that she had blatantly lied to him would put extra strain on an already strenuous journey. Kira already wondered how on earth they were supposed to capture and detain a King of Hell and hoped that Luke had a plan.

Luke had finished gathering supplies and handed a rucksack to Kira. He then held out a scabbard which housed a sword like nothing she had ever seen. It slid out of its holder with ease and was balanced to perfection. The sword was clearly sharp and despite the embellished hilt which was covered in onyx and sapphire stones, it was as light as a feather. She ran her fingers alongside and felt an etching on the blade although her eyes detected nothing, she supposed that it could have just been wear and tear if the sword had been used in battle.

With a sense of urgency, Luke assisted Kira in attaching the sword and scabbard to a brown leather belt that he slid around her waist. As he expertly fastened the belt, Kira couldn't help but feel grateful for having Luke by her side. She knew that without him, she would have been lost in this terrifying world of supernatural creatures. With her sword and scabbard securely attached to her, she felt much more confident and prepared to face whatever lay ahead.

Picking up the GPS, they both headed towards the dumbwaiter. Moving one by one, they ascended and returned to the main floor.

Consulting it, they realised that they were going to need a reliable vehicle to manoeuvre over the terrain in order to get to the King of Wrath. Kira knew that time was of the essence and that they couldn't afford to waste any time in getting there. With that in mind, they decided to search for a vehicle that could take them to their destination as quickly and as smoothly as possible. They set out to one of the strongholds garages, hoping that it was still intact and that they would soon find a vehicle that could take them where they needed to go.

As Kira and Luke looked around, they couldn't help but feel a sense of relief as the building remained empty. It was a rare moment of calmness amidst the chaos and danger of their lives. The only inhabitants of the building were the occasional wildlife that came to rummage through the wreckage. This gave Kira and Luke the much-needed break from battling demons and fighting for their lives.

Walking towards the garage, they discovered that the roof had collapsed, leaving only two of the walls remaining. Nestled at the back of the garage was a roofless safari jeep. On closer inspection, they noticed that one of the tires had been punctured by the collapse of the roof. Nevertheless, the spare tire housed at the rear of the jeep was intact. Luke skilfully set about replacing the tire, being careful not to disturb any of the wreckage, lest it cause the collapse of the two remaining walls.

Kira threw her rucksack into the back of the jeep and unfastened the belt, placing it at her side as she clambered into the passenger seat of the vehicle. Despite the challenges posed by the cramped space and the door blocked from fully extending due to the lack of available space., Luke squeezed into the driver's side of the jeep successfully.

As they settled into the jeep, Luke announced, 'Hold on!' before putting his foot down fully on the gas, revving the engine to the maximum. The goal was to plough over the debris and get on with their journey to their destination as quickly as possible. The torturous sound of the jeep's engine roaring like a monster echoed throughout the deserted garage as they made their way out.

Chapter Twenty

The smooth, well-paved roads and green countryside soon came to an end as the GPS navigated them through winding and narrow dirt lanes that cut through the mountains. The road had become rough terrain and driving became treacherous.

As they drove, Kira's thoughts turned to the looming confrontation with the King of Wrath. They had set out on this journey to hold him accountable for his people's crimes, and Kira hoped that the encounter would be amicable. However, given his name, she doubted that things would go smoothly.

Looking over at Luke, who was fixated on driving, Kira wondered if he was as nervous as she was about facing off against Wrath. In the back of her mind, she hoped that they had a solid plan in place for the eventuality that the King of Wrath was going to live up to his name.

As the sun began to set on the distant horizon, they knew that they had to be getting close, as the blue line on the GPS became shorter and shorter. There was no turning back now. With a deep breath, Kira steeled herself for what lay ahead, bracing herself for what could be their most dangerous encounter yet.

The GPS counted down to their destination as the air became thick with tension. Kira and Luke knew that they needed to approach the King of Wrath with political politeness. Should they wish to get him on board with accepting his people's crimes. Abandoning the vehicle, Luke and Kira would need to travel the remainder on foot as they approached a narrow opening which was fenced off with wood and barbed wire. The thick grass over-grown with wildflowers and weeds.

As Kira and Luke walked towards the fence, they could sense eyes on them. The air was tense with an unspoken hostility that made their hearts race. They knew that this meeting was going to be the most crucial of their lives.

As they continued to walk towards the gate, they could see that it was guarded by two heavily armed men who looked like they had seen more than their fair share of battles, with piercing red irises. The men eyed them suspiciously but finally allowed them to enter after checking their credentials.

The King of Wrath was not what Kira had imagined him to look like. He was chiseled with a strong jaw line and a light coating of stubble on his face. He was younger than she had expected, he only looked to be around 30. His eyes were a beautiful shade of violet, nothing like the creatures of his realm. His deep brown hair was formed into short curls that sat atop his head.

You would have said that he looked nothing like a demon except for the short, ram-style horns that protruded his head. Wrath hopped onto the wall and let his legs swing freely. He oozed a blasé care-free attitude. A light breeze wafted across, blowing Wrath's scent in the direction of Kira. The scent of vanilla mixed with cinnamon washed over her, drowning her senses... *How could someone so deadly, so dangerous, smell so sweet.*

Kira couldn't take her eyes off of Wrath. His dark hair seemed to shimmer slightly in the sunlight, giving him an otherworldly glow. His eyes were sharp and piercing, like they could see right through her.

As he approached her, she couldn't help but feel a thrill of excitement mixed with fear.

She knew she should be afraid, knew that he had the power to take her life in an instant, but there was something about him that drew her in.

She glanced down at her hands, which were trembling ever so slightly, and took a deep breath. She would not show weakness in front of him.

'Kira,' Wrath drawled, his voice smooth like honey, 'I've been looking for you.'

Kira's heart raced, but she kept her expression calm and composed. 'And what do you want with me?' she asked, trying to sound indifferent.

Wrath's lips curled up slightly into a smirk, 'Oh, just a little chat, my dear. No need to be so defensive. I promise I won't harm you... yet.'

Kira swallowed hard but held his gaze steadfastly. 'Fine. What do you want to talk about?'

Wrath sauntered closer to her, leaning in so close that she could feel his breath on her skin. Her heart fluttered in her chest, but she refused to back away.

'I want to talk about you.'

Luke coughed to get Wraths attention who was too busy focused on Kira. Luke was uneasy with the proximity between the pair and the control he seemed to have over Kira. Wrath turned in his direction, sizing Luke before gesturing that he could speak.

Kira was left standing there, her heart racing and her mind reeling. She knew that this was only the beginning of something much more dangerous...

Luke began to lecture Wrath, 'We are here to have you investigated for your people's crimes against humanity, the Wardens and my family. Not for some flirtatious, idle chit-chat'

'And to do so, your people sent you and the girl?' scoffed Wrath and he resumed his watch over Kira.

'Yes,' replied Luke, hoping that Wrath was unaware of his current strained relationship with the Wardens.

'I see. And you thought it best to approach this situation without acknowledging who you are speaking to.'

Luke infuriated with Wrath's hint at hierarchy, bit back, 'You are a King of Hell, you are not my King. I see no reason for undue formality.'

'Okay. So, no formality. Look, I'm going to level with you. I am tired of having the stupid seven-year cycle and I don't want to have to wait forty-two years for it to return back to my rule. Half a century is far too long and the Wrathlings don't want to wait any longer. The treaty is dated and no longer serves its purpose.

The world has changed. Evil is more common now than it has ever been. Surely you have seen that?'

Luke opened his mouth to speak but Wrath gestured for him to be silent.

'I get you are angry, and truly, I am sorry that a group of rogue Wrathlings attacked the stronghold. I am sorry that it resulted in the loss of your family. But that was not due to my command. You know how we operate. We only collect bad souls. So, I have nothing to be investigated for.'

Luke refused to remain quiet any longer and exploded with fury. 'Nothing? Nothing?!? Whether you meant them to or not. You were aware of their actions. Wrathlings, a lot more than a few rogues, have been killing people left, right and center. They are not doing their duty collecting bad souls. They have tried numerous times to kill us. Many of which, we narrowly escaped with our lives.'

Wrath continued with his blasé attitude and rolled his eyes. 'So, you want me to…punish them?'

Wrath clicked his fingers and announced proudly, 'Consider it done, all the ones responsible have been sent to the eternal abyss to live in eternal suffering and damnation.'

Wrath took off his jacket and swung it over one shoulder, with a smile he said, 'Well I must be off. Royal duties and all. Meet next week with the grand council to discuss rewriting the treaty laws? Kira, I will be seeing you for our chat.' Wrath's velvety voice caused Kira to shiver.

Luke was taken aback. *He really thinks that some stupid finger clicking is atonement for all of the crimes and deaths?*

Luke clenched his fists and firmly planted his feet, 'Woah. Not done pal. Far from it. We are taking you in to be put on trial for the crimes.'

Wrath laughed; a full belly-roaring laugh followed by a gasp for air. Wrath tried to say something but was unable to, as he tumbled to the ground. Luke rushed over to assess the situation. Wrath had been stabbed in the back of the head with a sharp blade emblazoned with unknown hieroglyphs. He was gone. Luke turned to Kira who was now ghostly pale, pointing. He followed her finger and found Wrath's attacker. The attacker smiled at him with a smile he knew all too well.

He whispered one word, '*Leon*'.

Chapter Twenty-One

As Luke recognized the attacker, a wave of anger coursed through him. Leon. He had always been a thorn in his family's side, causing trouble wherever he went. He was usually reckless, acting without thinking about the consequences but this was a whole new level. He had taken out the King of Wrath, making matters worse for everyone involved. He had committed treason.

Kira was equally shocked and visibly shaken, unable to speak. Luke took charge, grabbing Leon by the collar and lifting him up off the ground. 'What the hell is wrong with you? Why did you do this?' he demanded.

Leon's expression was smug, his eyes filled with malicious intent. 'I did it because he was weak. He was no true leader, only interested in his own selfish desires. I am here to claim the throne and rule over the Kingdom of Wrath as it was meant to be ruled.'

Luke could feel his anger build even further, but he maintained his composure. 'You have no right to claim anything. You are a criminal. You will face justice for what you have done.'

Leon merely laughed, pulling out his weapon and brandishing it threateningly. 'I don't think so. You are no match for me. I suggest you stand down and let me take what is mine.'

Leon turned to look directly at Kira, his face softening. 'Join me as my Queen, let us rule together. I meant what I said when I asked you to marry me, Kira. We were so good together; you know that to be true.'

Luke was about to respond when Kira suddenly stepped forward, her voice shaky but determined. 'No. Luke is right. You don't get to claim anything.'

Leon laughed at her, 'Luke always wanted what was mine. I see he has made a move on you.'

This angered Kira who clamped her hands into fists, 'You have no right to comment on anything. You disappeared. We thought you were dead!'

'And so, you what? Cried into my brother's arms?'

Luke stepped to Kira's side, 'You are way out of line. Don't try to turn this on me. You're the one who has just committed treason!'

'You don't realise it do you? Treason? No, No. It's a lot bigger than that. Who do you think set the wheels in motion for the Wrathling attacks? Who gave Wrath the idea to oppose the treaty? Oh brother, you really have no idea.'

'So, you put Kira through all of that. Faking your death? Risking her life for your hidden agenda. You are a giant…'

Kira interrupted Luke as she stormed towards Leon and slapped him square in his face. Leon rubbed his cheek, 'So that's how things are is it? My brother and my girl?'

Kira stood defiantly, 'I am not yours.' Not wanting to show that it really hurt her hand slapping him that hard.

'It hurts me that you think like that. We could have had it all… together. You could have been my Queen. It isn't too late Kira, just come with me. Forget my brother.'

'I am going nowhere with you. Your brother is twice the man that you are. I am glad you have shown your true colour before I said I do.'

Leon sneered, raising his weapon to strike. "So be it."

They had fought against their enemies alongside one another for many years and had always had each other's back. However, something about the way Leon treated Kira, perhaps it was the disrespect in his tone, or the fact that he had threatened her life, ignited an anger within Luke that he had never felt before. Despite their brotherly bond, Luke knew that he could not let this go, he had to stand up for Kira and for justice against his brother's actions. And so, with a heavy heart, he drew his sword and aimed it at Leon, fully prepared to engage in battle. It was a difficult decision, and one that he had not made lightly.

Within moments, the two brothers clashed swords, each determined to come out victorious. However, as they fought, there was a sense of sadness that hung in the air. This was not how they were meant to be, fighting against each other. They were supposed to be allies, two brothers fighting alongside one another against their enemies, not against each other.

Despite this, Luke knew that his actions were necessary. He couldn't just stand by and let Leon get away with everything. As the battle waged on, Luke could see the anger in his brother's eyes. Leon was consumed by his need for power.

Finally, after what felt like hours, the battle ended. Luke stood victorious, but he felt no satisfaction in his win. As he looked down at his defeated brother, he saw the sadness in his eyes, and Luke knew that this was not how things were meant to end.

In that moment, Luke knew that he had to make things right with his brother. He couldn't allow this battle to ruin their brotherly bond forever. They had always been a team; nothing was supposed to come between that - not even growing up and making their own choices.

And so, with a heavy heart, Luke extended his hand to Leon, offering to help him up. Leon rejected Luke's attempt to reconcile and showed disgust by spitting at him.

Leon's lust for power had consumed him entirely and it was at that moment that Luke realised he had lost his brother. His heart mourned for him a second time. Leon swung his legs and grappled at Luke's, bringing his brother to the ground. Leon grabbed his sword and went to strike as Kira came between them. She pleaded with Leon to stop. To turn himself in and not venture further down the dark path. Leon was blinded by his rage that he didn't even flinch at her words and instead went to deliver a final blow.

From afar, the sound of approaching footsteps echoed in the air as the Wardens closed in, charging towards the three individuals' location. Haruspex had called it in after a Wrathling had come to him to say that the King was dead. He didn't want the Wardens to come for him, after he handed over Wrath's location to Kira and Luke, so he came clean and offered to track them down in return for a pardon.

Leon pivoted his body, quickly turning his head towards the source of the approaching footsteps. He strained his ears to pick up any discernible sounds and averted his gaze towards the peripheral of his vision, trying to identify any suspicious movements. His instincts told him that trouble was brewing, and he wasn't about to take any chances. He withdrew his sword and remarked, 'This isn't over,' before cutting the air with a jewelled blade, a glowing tear appeared as if the knife had cut through the air. He jumped through it, disappearing, leaving the two alone in the clearing with Wraths body continuing to grow cold.

As the Wardens finally arrived at the location, they wasted no time in drawing out their weapons and displaying them, their steely glares fixed upon Kira and Luke. Their voices rang out clear and unequivocally, demanding that the duo turn themselves in immediately.

Tensions escalated as the two parties faced each other down, with the Wardens' weapons serving as a warning of the consequences and severity of the situation. Kira and Luke exchanged a worried glance, weighing their options carefully as the Wardens showed no signs of backing down.

Chapter Twenty-Two

As the Wardens edged nearer and began circling around Kira and Luke, the duo realised they had no choice but to turn themselves in. The Wardens' weapons remained pointed and engaged, and the tense situation did nothing to ease Kira and Luke's apprehensions. Despite their reluctance, they knew that they had to face the impending consequences of their actions. They had failed to get Wrath to admit to the Wrathlings wrongdoings and to hold him accountable. Then they had failed to capture Leon.

With heavy hearts and a sinking feeling in their stomachs, they started to move slowly towards the Wardens, their hands raised in apparent surrender. The Wardens continued to maintain their vigilance, and it was clear that they weren't about to lower their weapons anytime soon. Luke and Kira were placed in handcuffs and escorted back to an armoured vehicle. Adrastus stood outside the vehicle, disappointment plastered across his face. He had always viewed Luke as a son and now, all he felt was betrayal.

When the pair arrived at the vehicle Adrastus folded his arms and began scolding Luke, 'You have disgraced the Ward name. Your parents would be tossing in their graves right now. You have gone too far Luke and there is nothing that I can do for you now. You will be put on trial. Both of you for the actions you have taken and for the treason you have committed in killing a crowned King of Hell. If you didn't realise before the gravity of the situation, here it is…You two have just unleashed a whole lot of ugly and an impending war'.

Luke looked as if all the air in his lungs had been sucked out of him. Adrastus's words stung. Kira refused to allow him to be bullied any longer.

'Adrastus, Luke has done nothing but be honourable and adhered to every rule you have set. We didn't kill the King of Wrath, Leon did.

But you scared him off before we could bring him in!'

Adrastus pushed his tongue to the roof of his mouth, as if he had swallowed something distasteful, he spat each word out, 'You. You are the reason for all of this. You have destroyed his life. Luke was one of the greatest Wardens we had ever had and you. I don't know whether you bewitched him or what, but you are a danger to humanity and will be treated as such. The fact that you dare to put the blame on a fallen Warden is atrocious. You dare to speak ill of the dead. Take them away.'

As he said the last part, he gestured to two Wardens who were wearing clothes made of chainmail their heads covered by thick black helmets.

The pair, Kira and Luke, found themselves directed towards the back of the armoured vehicle, their apprehension mounting as they were ushered inside. The interior was cramped and unwelcoming, with no windows or means of escape apparent. They sat down on the hard metal bench, and the door was slammed shut behind them, sealing them off from the outside world.

The roar of the engine and the sound of the wheels on the rough terrain added to their unease, as they wondered what would happen next. The darkness inside the vehicle seemed to stretch out forever, broken only by the occasional unsympathetic jolt as the vehicle navigated the terrain. Kira and Luke exchanged worried glances, both wondering how they had ended up in this situation and what kind of fate awaited them at the end of this journey. The only thing they knew for certain was that they were currently not in control, and that their future was very much in the hands of the Wardens who had taken them into custody.

Luke sat defeated, his head hung low and his spirit broken. Kira, on the other hand, refused to give up hope. She sat next to Luke, deep in thought, trying to come up with a plan to get them out of the situation. She knew it would be risky, but at this point, it was their best chance for survival. Her mind raced as she considered their options.

She knew that if they could somehow create a distraction, they might be able to overpower the Wardens and make a run for it. But she knew it would be a long shot. She would need to act quickly, without hesitation, and use all of her wits and cunning to outsmart their captors. As the armoured vehicle bounced along the rough terrain, Kira's mind was working overtime, trying to piece together a plan for escape. She studied the doors, the small openings, and any other weaknesses that might give them a chance.

Kira, determined to take control of their situation, thought hard about their options. The more she analysed their situation, the more she realised that their only chance of escape would be to get the Wardens to open the doors. Once the doors were open, they would need to exert force and overpower the Wardens to make their escape. A risky plan, but it was their only option. Kira knew they couldn't just sit and wait for fate to decide their future.

They needed to act and create an opportunity to escape. She considered a few ideas, weighing the pros and cons of each, and finally settled on a plan that seemed feasible. To get the Wardens to open the doors, they would need to create a scene, something that would force them to stop the vehicle and investigate.

Kira began to think about what would distract them and how they could implement it. It was a dangerous plan, and the risks were high, but she knew it was their only hope. With newfound determination and a sense of purpose, Kira began to lay out her plan, ready to act when the opportunity presented itself. The only real problem would be getting Luke onboard without the Wardens knowing.

Kira just had to hope that Luke would get the jist and understand what was going on. Hopefully, he would go with it, otherwise they were stuck.

Kira screamed, 'I hate you!'

Luke jolted and looked directly at her. 'What the hell?'

'You! This is all your fault! I wish I had never met you!' her voice venomous.

Luke was stumped, 'You don't mean that'.

'Oh, but I do! My life is ruined because of you. Oh, how I wish my hands were free to strangle the living daylights out of you. I hate you so damn much!'

Luke was hurt, his mind processing her words, except they didn't feel like her words. Then his mind clicked.

'Yeah well, I hate you! My whole family is dead because of you. You are a dangerous and vile woman.'

The pair continued to shout hateful remarks getting louder each time. One of the Wardens banged on the metal wall from the front cabin.

'Will you both just shut up! Don't make me come back there!'

Kira screamed back, 'I won't stop until I am far away from him! I can't stand looking at his face any longer.'

Her heart raced with excitement as the vehicle finally came to a halt. This was their chance. She had spent the last couple of hours meticulously planning their escape, and now it was time to put that plan into action. Kira signalled to Luke to get ready. She knew that every second was precious, and they needed to move quickly. With a deep breath and a sense of urgency, Kira sprang into action.

As the Wardens stepped out of the vehicle to investigate, Kira and Luke launched their surprise attack. The Wardens had no idea what was happening, Luke using his free legs to kick and fight against them, and the Wardens were quickly overpowered. Kira knew they couldn't waste any time, so she sprinted towards the door, threw it open, and bolted past the remaining guards.

Luke snatched the keys to the handcuffs as they ran past. They ran as fast as they could, using every ounce of strength they had left to put distance between themselves and their captors. They knew they were not out of danger yet and had to live a life on the run. Hoping that somehow, amends could be made and if they could prove that Leon was behind it all. Maybe they wouldn't have to run any longer.

They had travelled for days and had finally took up a spot in a little village. With little money and means to go by they had to rely on Luke's powers of persuasion to get food, drink, and shelter. However, this was short-lived as Warden scouts were spotted. They narrowly avoided detection, but it signalled that it was time to move on.

They travelled for weeks, through thick forests and rugged terrain, never staying in one place for too long.

One evening, as they set up camp on the banks of a river, Luke had caught a fish and was attempting to start a fire, the weather proving to be against them. Kira felt a tingling sensation flow through her body, her fingertips buzzing. Without thinking, she reached out towards the stack of kindling, sticks, and leaves, and her fingers grazed the pile's edges, causing a sudden and magnificent violet flame to ignite. The purple flames dancing against the rain and wind. Refusing to be put out. Luke looked at Kira, who was mesmerised by the flames that were trailing from her fingertips to the logs below.

'Did you know you could do that?' he asked.

'I. I've gotten these feelings a few times where I thought I saw sparks and I think I incinerated the Wrathlings at Ground Zero. But I don't actually know what it is. It just happens.'

She watched as the flames interweaved between her fingers. Wrapping themselves around like a serpent made of flames.

Chapter Twenty-Three

For weeks, Nira had been on the trail of Kira and Luke. The world had gone on high alert ever since the news of the King of Wrath's murder had been announced. The bounty for the pair's capture was substantial, and every stronghold was on the lookout. Nira knew that this was not going to be an easy task, but she was determined to find them before anyone else did.

Growing up, Nira had been close to Luke and his family. She knew that Luke was an incredibly skilled fighter and that he was loyal to his cause. She couldn't believe that he would have done something as drastic as breaking the treaty, but the evidence against him was overwhelming. Nevertheless, Nira was not willing to give up on her old friend just yet.

She had heard whispers of Kira and Luke's movements across various districts and had been tracking them through urban jungles, across barren wastelands, and through dense forests. She had witnessed their skill in avoiding detection, always being one step behind. Nira had to be shrewd and smart if she had any hope of catching them.

As she inched closer to their location, Nira's heart raced with anticipation. She knew that this was the moment she had been preparing for. The terrain became rougher as Nira approached the warehouse. Her footsteps became quieter as she slipped into the shadows, scanning her surroundings for any sign of Kira and Luke. They were in an abandoned factory on the outskirts of the city. The walls were covered in peeling paint, and the air was thick with the smell of dust and rust.

As she moved forward, Nira could hear the faint sound of footsteps nearby. Creeping, her foot hit something, and she felt a tug. Her body propelled into the air surrounded by a net. She sucked in her breath, Her weapon was tightly lodged to her side and as she was unable to utilise it she feared for the worst. But as the figures emerged from the shadows, Nira's heart leapt with relief. It was Kira and Luke, their faces strained but resolute.

Nira knew that their encounter was not going to be easy, but she had to do what was right. She explained her reason for being there and her belief in their cause. She wanted to help them clear their names and bring peace to the kingdoms once again.

Kira and Luke looked at each other, their expressions unreadable. But Nira knew that her words had struck a chord. She waited patiently for their response, knowing that the outcome of this encounter would be crucial for them all.

Kira extended her arm and revealed a small blade which she used to cut the rope that was holding Nira up in the air. Nira plummeted to the ground with a resounding thud. She was thankful for the release however she couldn't help but rub at her sides as a result of the fall.

Kira helped Nira to her feet and guided her towards a pile of old crates.
'Are you okay?' she asked, searching Nira's face for any signs of injury.

Nira nodded, a small smile forming on her lips. Luke approached his old friend and smiled, his eyes then caught a glimpse of her loaded weapon and the smile faded.

Disappointed, Luke muttered, 'I see you are here for business. Was what you said, a lie?'

Nira frowned, 'It really isn't like that Luke.'

'Then which is it? Are you here to help us or are you against us?'

'You think if I was against you, that I would have come alone?'

Luke paused, his shoulders relaxing. 'I've missed you,' he said as he embraced Nira in a tight hug.

'I've missed you too. But a lot has happened since the King's death and I'm not sure how much of it you are aware of.'

Luke shrugged, 'I know we are on the run and wanted by every Warden and Wrathling for his murder. But I can't say I know of anything else, given I don't have time to watch the news.'

'Let's just say. The King's death is the least of our concerns and the grand council are trying to cover themselves by pressing the focus on you two. The other six sins have awoken and they're all arguing over who gets to rule the Kingdom of Wrath. They also want your heads too. As a result of all of this, the whole of Hell is now in uproar and because the leaders are too busy arguing, the demons from each realm are running riot and it's just a total mess.'

Luke sighed, 'Great. Is there anyone who doesn't want our heads?'

Nira continued, 'Nope. But that's not all. His key is missing.'

Kira piped up, 'A key?'

Nira sighed, her face lowered, 'Wrath's key to his kingdom. Whoever possesses it is rightfully the ruler of the kingdom.'

Kira and Luke exchanged looks, as if somehow, they were communicating non-verbally. Nira, who was clearly not privy to the conversation between the pair, spoke up, 'Anything you wish to share with little old me?'

Luke looked directly at Nira, 'We now know what Leon will be going after.'

'Leon? He's dead…' she stopped herself before adding, 'isn't he?'

Kira answered with a clear and resounding, 'No.'

'And you think he will be going after the key? Is that what you are suggesting?' quizzed Nira as she processed the news that her fallen comrade was indeed alive and was not the innocent and tragic loss that the Wardens had made out.

The pair, entirely in sync announced, 'We know so.'

Nira, trying to lighten the mood spoke in a hopeful tone, 'Well, we better find it first. Any suggestions on how?'

Luke's face grew cold,

'We speak to a demon friend of ours.'

*Kira and Luke
will return in...*

The Seven Levels of Sin:
Flame

Spring 2024

'Flame'
Preview

Chapter One

…and with the fire, all shall burn…
-Book of the Ancient Artefacts-

Nira had been following the news that the main Warden stronghold had been decimated by the Wrathlings. She had been close friends with Luke when they were both in training. But things had happened and over the years the pair had gone their separate ways. Still the news that his family's stronghold had been attacked tugged at her heart strings. She had hoped that there would be news of survivors but according to what the elders of the European stronghold were discussing, it was incredibly unlikely. There had even been reports that the Wrathlings had captured the souls of Luke's parents.

Nira felt a deep sense of sadness and guilt wash over her as she remembered the last time she had seen Luke. They had been on a mission together and Nira had disobeyed orders, putting both of their lives in danger. Luke had been furious with her, and they had parted ways on bad terms. She had always regretted her actions but never had the chance to apologise and make things right.

Now, as she stood among the elders of the European stronghold, Nira knew that she needed to do something. She couldn't change what had happened to Luke's family, but she could try to make amends with him. She asked the elders if they had any information on Luke's whereabouts and was told that he had been spotted in the nearby town and that a group of Wardens had been sent to go after him and bring him in.

Without hesitation, Nira set off towards the town. Her heart was racing with anticipation and nervousness as she made her way through the crowded streets. Turning corners as she came head on with a warehouse. She stumbled as the terrain changed underfoot but regained her balance quickly. She couldn't afford to make a mistake. She owed this to Luke.

She had entered an abandoned factory. The walls rotted and worn, covered with layers of dust, rust and peeling paint. Nira turned; she could hear footsteps nearby. Creeping towards where the footsteps were coming from her foot caught on something and she was thrown into the air, caught up in a large net. She sucked in her breath, her weapon was tightly lodged to her side, unable to utilise it she feared for the worst. But as the figures emerged from the shadows, Nira's heart leapt with relief. It *was* Kira and Luke, their faces hard to read. But Luke didn't seem to be all that pleased.

Nira knew that this was not going to be easy, but she had to do what was right. She explained her reason for being there and her belief in their cause. She wanted to help them clear their names and bring peace to the kingdoms once again. Nira had to hope that Luke realised how sincere she was and how she was on their side in spite of what the council thought about them.

Kira and Luke looked at each other, their expressions silently communicating their thoughts. But Nira knew that her words had struck a chord as Kira's face softened. She waited patiently for their response, knowing that the outcome of this encounter would be crucial.

Kira extended her arm and revealed a small blade which she used to cut the rope that was holding Nira up in the air. Nira plummeted to the ground with a resounding thud. She was thankful for the release however she couldn't help but rub at her sides as a result of the fall.

Kira helped Nira to her feet and guided her towards a pile of old crates. 'Are you okay?' she asked, searching Nira's face for any signs of injury.

Nira nodded, a small smile forming on her lips. Luke approached his old friend and smiled, his eyes then caught a glimpse of her loaded weapon and the smile faded. Disappointed, Luke muttered, 'I see you are here for business. Was what you said a lie?' Nira frowned, 'It really isn't like that Luke.'

'Then which is it? Are you here to help us or are you against us?'

'You think if I was against you, that I would have come alone?'

Luke paused, his shoulders relaxing. 'I've missed you,' he said as he embraced Nira in a tight hug.

'I've missed you too. But a lot has happened since the King's death and I'm not sure how much of it you are aware of.'

Luke shrugged, 'I know we are on the run and wanted by every Warden and Wrathling for his murder. But I can't say I know of anything else, given I don't have time to watch the news.'

'Let's just say. The King's death is the least of our concerns and the grand council are trying to cover themselves by pressing the focus on you two. The other six sins have awoken and they're all arguing over who gets to rule the Kingdom of Wrath. They also want your heads too. As a result of all of this, the whole of Hell is now in uproar and because the leaders are too busy arguing, the demons from each realm are running riot and it's just a total mess.'

Luke sighed, 'Great. Is there anyone who doesn't want our heads?'

'Nope. But that's not all. His key is missing.'

'A key?'

'Wrath's key to his kingdom. Whoever possesses it is rightfully the ruler of the kingdom.'

Kira and Luke exchanged looks. Nira, who was clearly not privy to the conversation between the pair, spoke up, 'Anything you wish to share with little old me?'

'We now know what Leon will be going after.'

'Leon? He's dead…' she stopped herself before adding, 'isn't he?'

Kira answered as if the word left a distaste in her mouth, 'No.'

'And you think he will be going after the key? Is that what you are suggesting?'

'We know so.'

Nira, trying to lighten the mood spoke in a hopeful tone, 'Well, we better find it first. Any suggestions on how?'

Luke's face grew cold, 'We speak to a demon friend of ours.'

'Luke, I'm so sorry about what happened between us,' Nira finally blurted out. 'I know that I messed up and put both of our lives in danger. If I could go back in time and fix things, I would.'

Luke's expression softened as he listened to her words. 'Nira, it's okay. I've long since forgiven you for what happened. We were both young and reckless back then. What matters now is that we're both here, fighting for the same cause.'

Nira felt a weight lift off her shoulders as she heard Luke's words. They spent the next few hours catching up on old times, discussing the news of the decimated stronghold, how to speak to Haruspex and strategising on how best to fight back against the Wrathling threat. For the first time in a long time, Nira felt a sense of hope and purpose. She knew that she had an ally in Luke and Kira. That as a team, they could make a difference. Just like the good old days. Fighting together against threats to humanity.

Chapter Two

The now trio had concocted a plan to get the ingredients they would need to summon Haruspex. It was risky but it was the only shot they had.

Nira played lookout for any Warden scouts or Wrathlings that may come hunting whilst Kira and Luke sought to their unusual shopping list. They were going to have to do things the ancient way and instead of fancy bottles of various oils and liquids they were going to have to channel darker magic.

Luke had only ever seen this once whilst in training. A higher-level Warden, a member of the council, was the one that conducted the demonic ceremony. Thankfully, Luke had an incredible memory and remembered most of the ingredients with Nira adding on the last one. He was thankful that Nira was here to lend a hand. Hell knows they could use all of the help that they could get. They collected various herbs and flowers; wolfsbane, verbena, mint, lavender and carnation. Then they sourced snake blood which unfortunately isn't common and required a live animal to sacrifice to get the ingredient they required. Kira and Luke headed to the local pet-shop and found a very sad owner. He told the pair that he had sadly just lost a milk snake, so he needed to shut up shop to take the animal to the vet to find out why it had passed away as it was perfectly healthy and young just hours before. Luke used persuasion to retrieve the milk snake, thankful that he wouldn't have to harm a live animal.

With the ingredients collected, they headed back to the warehouse and Nira arrive d shortly after. She was happy to report that there had been no sightings of Wrathlings or Wardens. Relieved, they set about making a pentagram on the floor using a tin of old paint. Placing the ingredients into the middle of the pentagram. Luke pulled out a dagger.

'You know what comes next,' he said as he handed Nira the dagger. She made a slice length ways on Luke's finger, allowing the blood to trickle over the collected ingredients. Then came Niras turn, again blood trickled over. Finally came Kira's turn. She hesitated at first but understood that it wouldn't work unless everyone involved in the summoning sacrificed a few drops of blood. She winced as the blade sliced through her skin, her blood pooling on the surface until it finally ran down and dropped to the floor.

Luke and Nira stood at either end of the pentagram, careful to not step within the circle. They began chanting, 'Demone ti chiamiamo, vieni avanti e parlaci.' The chanting grew louder as the pentagram ebbed and glowed. Violet coloured light shone from the centre. Smoke bellowing and swirling. Darkness consumed all of the light in the warehouse. The trio stood still. The chanting stopped.

Suddenly, a shadowy figure started to emerge from the smoke. Luke didn't want to waste any time, so he looked at Kira and Nira, they both agreed.

'We seek your knowledge,' said Luke, bravely stepping forward. 'We need your help.'

The figure laughed, a cold, humourless sound that echoed through the empty warehouse. 'And what makes you think I would help you? You have disturbed my rest and brought me back to this realm.'

'We had no other choice. You're the last person I want to see Haruspex, believe me.'

'Haruspex?' smiled Wrath, his eyes shimmering with a menacing glint.

*Kira and Luke
will return in...*

The Seven Levels of Sin:
Flame

Spring 2024

Want to get the latest news on future releases
by S.L. Pearce?

Follow Sian Pearce on Instagram, Facebook
or TikTok

www.slpearce.com

ABOUT THE AUTHOR

S.L. PEARCE is a United Kingdom resident who has nurtured a lifelong passion for reading and storytelling. Their deep fascination with narrative and world-building culminated in the completion of their debut fantasy novel, "The Seven Levels of Sin: Spark".

Through this work, S.L. PEARCE expertly weaves together elements of the supernatural, action, and adventure to create a thrilling and engaging tale that takes readers on an unforgettable journey. With an eye for detail and a flair for imaginative writing, S.L. PEARCE is sure to captivate readers around the world.

Milton Keynes UK
Ingram Content Group UK Ltd.
UKHW010756110923
428455UK00014B/604